Rescue Me

Rescue Me

MEGAN CLARK

KENSINGTON BOOKS
http://www.kensingtonbooks.com

KENSINGTON BOOKS are published by

Kensington Publishing Corp.
850 Third Avenue
New York, NY 10022

ISBN 0-7582-0980-0

First Kensington Trade Paperback Printing: July 2005
10 9 8 7 6 5 4 3 2 1

Printed in the United States of America

For Ava

Acknowledgments

I offer gratitude to my editor, Audrey LaFehr, for her careful readings and literary insights about this novel and the subject matter; Angela Rinaldi, my wonderful agent, who because of her expertise and intuition was able to guide me through to the finish and found me the right home for this story; for my writer's group (especially Elaura Niles), for all your support along the way; and to my friendly readers and editors whose intuition I so trust—Nancy Hardin (my guardian angel), Heather Marcroft, Jessica Morrell and Frances Hwang; Lisa Oshop, for the compliment that kept me going; James Ragan, Sid Stebel, Kate Trueblood, Steven Vanderstaay, Tom Spanbauer and The Dangerous Writers, who taught me how to live on paper; my muses—Nichole, Bridgette and, always, Julia; Robin Laws, for her maternal support and encouragement to always go deeper; Jim and Susan Engberg, my life rafts; Annie Erneaux and William S. Burroughs—whose experimental prose dare me to be different; George Clark Jr., who taught me artistic endurance; George Clark Sr., for looking out for my best; Donald Smith, for supporting my European dreams; Joy Carriger, for being there in her sparkly way; Hedgebrook, a wonderful writing residency which nurtured me for three weeks of uninterrupted bliss; Jim and Sharon Bortnem, whose loyalty I will never forget; Brad Bortnem, my dear friend and mentor, who encouraged me to complete this project and whose devotion to my growth changed my life—without him this book would never have been written; Andy Buzan, my great muse, whose love and passion continuously inspire me; and most especially, a loving universe that rewards loving labor.

And the day came when the risk it took to remain tight inside the bud was more painful than the risk it took to blossom.

—Anaïs Nin

Chapter 1

Sunspots

"*Needs more variety*," the comment read, scrawled in red ink. "*Can't see your range.*"

Beneath her comment, my professor had drawn a big "C" on the cover of my portfolio, indicating my grade for the semester. When I had started the program, I knew that becoming an artist had nothing to do with grades, yet the personal comment about my "lack of range" still stung. I quickly zipped the leather portfolio case shut and began to walk along one of UCLA's many shortcuts toward the campus café.

I was on my way to meet my summer roommates, strangers with whom I would soon be sharing intimate space while attending a poetry program in Prague. Although I had no background in poetry or writing, I was drawn to Prague for the sheer aesthetic of its reputation. Not only did the architectural images I'd seen in magazines of Prague carry a decadence that was unavailable in the States, but I'd been captivated by its nickname boasted on the program flyer: "Tour Prague— *The Velvet City.*" The idea of a city with texture both fascinated and disturbed me and seemed almost taboo—a city I could brush my skin against.

Students had been grouped into trios, and we'd been advised in an orientation letter to get acquainted with each other as early as possible. I didn't know Valerie or Natasha, who were both students in the writing department, even though the photography department was only one building away. We'd scheduled a meeting for this afternoon—four weeks before our departure.

Sunlight radiated through the thick cathedral windows of Old Main Hall and filtered through the maples and palm trees, creating a latticework of light against my clothes. The heat penetrated through to my skin and I began to perspire. I took a long quiet breath, trying to release the anticipation from my chest. Worry had a way of making me feel outside of myself, all too known and exposed, like a reverse negative. Two women who were now strangers would soon be dreaming and dressing and writing poetry next to me.

I slipped on my sunglasses and watched the ground as I walked.

As a photographer, I knew aperture settings, film speed, shadow effects, and contrasting tones. I knew how to control the speed of my life with photographs, how to make the darkness seem lighter, and how to manipulate an image. I didn't know what it was to look into someone's eyes and surrender, to be taken away from all I'd known. I lived under the assumption that if I combed my hair just right, or scrubbed my face harder, there would be some great payoff in the end, and that my life would become more interesting. My relationship with Grant, which had been going on the last six months, was a flat satisfaction; nothing less than consistent, and yet, disappointingly, nothing more. I had read somewhere that the definition of insanity was when a person repeated the same things over and over again, yet expected a different result. I needed this summer to be different—a meandering surprise. If only I could simply learn how to kill the routine. Let go of all I knew. Find out what would happen with the net gone and the safety off. Who would I be then? Would this summer tell me?

I walked beneath an umbrella of palm trees. We'd had a dry spell and grass crackled beneath my feet. Summer was racing up to me, and everywhere flowers were already stripped of bloom. Los Angeles has a way of fast-forwarding the seasons and making barren even the most fertile times. It had its own clock—a cousin to Mother Nature who ran things, probably a male. I could taste the air; salty and toxic like glue or semen.

This was the death awaiting me if I didn't start living soon.

Yesterday, I arrived at Grant's apartment, knowing every inch the privileged young woman I was, but feeling rather half empty. Did it matter if Grant greeted me with showering affections, drew me a bath, and laid me against freshly washed sheets? Whether it was standing in the hallway, floating in a pool of jasmine-scented water, or lying in his bed, I knew the landscape of our passion, the height of its peaks, and afterwards, when I returned home, slightly damp and always a little light-headed, the depths of its lonely valleys.

I had anticipated that I would soon want to depart from Grant, only to change my mind the second I faced him. He satisfied me physically and I took to him rather unconsciously as some people might to a habit of snacking in their sleep, later waking to a kitchen riddled with crumbs.

A warm hug. Smells of freshly showered skin. Hair brushed neatly back and still slightly wet. Grant greeted me in his usual fashion. In his hold, I searched for body scent as though wanting to find another man; beneath his arms, at the swell of his chest, behind his ears. I had grown used to finding, instead, a vacancy, or rather, a crispness. His lack of smelling like tobacco or beer or even the slight residue of natural musk warned me: I could never fall in love with a man who had no scent of his own.

I'd even grown used to his listless apartment, lacking girly posters, empty bottles, or displays of music and movies that were otherwise so typical of college men, projecting fantasies of the lives they desired (and which would most likely never transpire) but that nevertheless created some character. I had grown used to most things in my life because the idea of demanding what I wanted from life seemed inconceivable. I simply accepted what was given to me.

"I aced my finals," Grant said. He was a dedicated student of biology with plans of being a dentist.

I made myself smile. "You're so tenacious. Your family will be proud."

Grant took me by the waist and pulled me closer, my backpack dropping to the floor with a thump. His hand glided along the back of my shirt as he kissed me. "Sometimes I wonder what it is we have here," he said.

It was the first time either of us had attempted to define our relationship. We were standing in the doorway. I wore a T-shirt and jeans, he shorts. We both stared at the floor, waiting for my response.

I didn't have one.

He took me by the chin with his hand and drew my face towards his. "You don't have to respond to that," he said, his breath minty. "I'm just thinking out loud tonight."

His trusting blue eyes looked away, back at the floor.

"I'm going to miss this," he said.

I assumed that his thoughts referred to our sex life. We hardly spent any time together. Our six months had been a breeze, nothing much more than an evening or two per week. I wondered if he wanted to see other people.

He reached down and buried his face into the belly of my shirt, his hands sliding underneath it. As though to push him away, I instantly brought my hands to his head, wanting to resist his efforts for once, but my body betrayed me, already beginning to arch towards his. My navel was instantly warmed by his tongue. My hands clawed through his mass of dark blond hair, and I began to breathe deeply. Leaning into me, I felt his erection press against my jeans, my insides becoming moist in anticipation. I abandoned the rest of my clothing right there in the hall.

He drew me a warm bath and I slipped into the water with routine-like duty, quick to get it over with. Although the gesture was concerted as one of generous hospitality, I intuited Grant's central purpose for the bath as one which paralleled his own standards: he wanted me sterilized before sex.

Between my legs the heat entered me, marking me more so by what it took from me, rather than what it left. I floated aimlessly from side to side in the small porcelain tub, feeling wooden.

I fantasized a slimy purple and green pond to bury my genitals into.

"Do it now," I demanded.

My feet had found a place to rest on his muscular calves, which supported most of the weight of my body.

"What's the hurry?"

I became self-conscious for a moment. "I just want you," I whispered.

Grant closed his eyes and pressed his lips against mine, drawing me in more tightly with his tongue. Our tongues collided and melded into one another's mouths in the seamless way our bodies melded together: like caressing mirror images of ourselves. I predicted Grant's breath, the tilt of his face, and the tongue that encircled my lips and pulled back softly, relaxing into the consistency of the kiss as though I were sleeping, dreaming a smooth, recurring dream.

We were lying on his bed. He had lit a white candle on his nightstand and the lights were off. The room was cool from the air conditioner and although I would have liked a cover, I resisted the blanket in order to allow Grant the favor of watching our bodies in the candlelight.

Through the outside of his cotton shorts, my hand caressed him.

"Danielle," he said, bringing my chin up again so that I could meet his gaze. "I think this might be love."

His vagueness eased me and I could not help but respond to him physically. I unlatched his belt. It amazed me how hard I could make him by just unzipping his pants. This wasn't an act of reciprocated love, not an escape into him, but through him.

"You're wild," he said. "I had no idea when we first met that you would be so wild."

"With you I am," I whispered, pulling off his shorts.

In some ways, I regretted my wildness. I wondered why I couldn't be satisfied with making sweet, calm love like so many others seemed to. To find a resting point seemed impossible and I avoided the silences by talking with my body.

And then she appeared. *Mother.* In my mind. Applauding

the relationship she had approved of from the start. After all, Grant had those gentlemanly qualities that were time-tested favorites. He would have been accepted centuries ago to mothers across the world. Sometimes my memory told me that Mother had introduced Grant to me initially, set us up, but this was more or less my emotional memory. We had met, in fact, online. Our chance meeting was nothing more than electronic. We were an electronic match. We embodied a calculated passion.

I tried my best to clear Mother from my mind and refocus on Grant. The hair on his thighs was coarse and dark blond, like his pubic hair. In his plaid boxers, his length stood against the material, as if waiting to be released. I pulled him outside of his shorts, my lips enwrapping his smoothness. I began to lick him up and down, softly at first, and then hard until I could not help but swallow him into my entire mouth. His skin was tasteless and firm, quivering at each of my caresses. Grant gasped, "Yeah, Danielle. That's so good."

My heartbeat began to build and I started to sweat a little.

It was his turn now to go down on me. Either side of my thighs was fondled with his lips until, between them, I became wet again and loosened beneath his mouth as his tongue broke past my web of pubic hair and into me. He licked back and forth, with vigorous speed. I arched my back as he pushed my legs open wider and inserted two fingers into my wetness. I could feel my buttocks flex.

"What are you waiting for?" I said.

"Not yet," he whispered, and continued, his saliva drenching me.

We formed a sixty-nine position so that we could stroke

and taste each other at the same time. I savored his length as it slid against the back of my throat, the tip of his penis the most delicate ridge for me to massage and lick and rouse to full measure. His legs spread slightly. I enjoyed manipulating him, grazing this area of his body with my breath, rubbing the swells below his sex while I sucked him. His body winced passionately above my head.

His tongue began to feel like sex. I yearned to feel him inside me and wondered when it would happen. Finally he gave in to desire and I felt the long-awaited emptiness fill with instant calm. He took me by the waist and turned me about, forcing his body on top of mine, his heat penetrating me. I rotated my hips and pulled them forward and back, feeling him enter and exit at my will. Grant stopped rocking and asked me if I liked it.

"More than you know," I whispered. "Keep going!"

I wrapped my legs around him and pressed until he was as deep inside me as possible. The thought occurred to me that this was as close as we could ever get. This naked place was all we really had.

We glided back and forth until I climaxed. It happened in a wave of blurry emotion as I gazed about his bedroom, looking from side to side at shapes in the room barely lit by the miniature flame, feeling watched by something other than him, gripping his erection with my inner thigh muscles. He thrust again and again, making me climax by just pressing my stomach and penetrating me at once. I ran my hands through my own head of blond hair until, not knowing any alternative or what else to do with the pleasure I felt, I fell onto his chest with a gasp.

He surprised me by grabbing my calves and raising my legs high, spreading them into a V, his stomach muscles flexing as he shook me to and fro. I could barely take the pressure of his sex, although I resisted complaining. I liked feeling overwhelmed. I ran my hand along his back, just below his neck, and slid my fingers along the sweat that had gathered along his spine. His chest heaved in and out as he breathed fiercely, his neck and face reddening. He was getting close.

I scurried off the bed and kneeled, pulling Grant's legs to the edge of the mattress so that I could please him in his most favorite fashion—with my mouth.

It did not take him long to come. At last he let out a long, beautiful moan. There was a tenderness to him that made me think of how a woman might sound during lovemaking.

After a pause, I swallowed, then let my mouth rest around his engorged cock, feeling his length quiver and throb until it lay wet and tired against my tongue.

When it was over, it was over. Back to suburbia. We were the reflection of something common, having freshly come against ourselves, pink, temporarily satisfied. Was there more to relationships than this?

A waterfall of caresses, kisses and sweat rolling down the cliffs of our young golden bodies—a static shot, a lifeless stream flowing nowhere. We were a facade of vitality and movement, silently fixed.

Our relationship was not unlike a photo of nature, by no means a substitute for what should have been profound and vitally felt. But in the framework of my small life, it looked good.

We were, somehow, equal.

The campus café was located at the top of a long set of stairs. Near the entrance an American flag hung limp in spite of the slight breeze. Sounds of papers shuffling, backpacks being shouldered and unshouldered, and ringing phones

filled the building as I entered. Female voices echoed in the
hallway like thoughts, punctuated by shrills of laughter and
sneakers pivoting to a screech.

I stopped at the top of the stairs. Absentmindedness
plagued my family, so I made it a point to try to remember
whether today was yesterday or tomorrow. Three choices on
random spin. One day blurring into the next. But today felt
like today. I knew where I was and why I was. But I couldn't
remember how in the hell I'd found the courage to sign the
papers to study abroad. In fact, I could barely remember anything except that I was about to meet two strange women
whom I would be spending my summer with. I started toward the tables, now with uncharacteristic intention, shoulders back and chin up. I nearly smiled.

I immediately spotted Natasha, seated alone. Yesterday she
had answered the phone, "Good news, please?" These had
been her first words, and they hung in the air, both an invitation and a suit of armor. It was easy to spot her now in the
teal scarf she said she'd be wearing. Like a costumed actress
offstage, she had an open expression, her eyes wide, as though
anxious to take on a dramatic role. She looked over at me curiously and waved, her brows raised.

"You're Danielle?" she asked, as I slid into the chair opposite her.

I nodded and set my portfolio at my feet.

Our other roommate hadn't showed yet. Natasha was
looking at me, somewhat puzzled. Technically, the description
I had given of myself ("tall, thin, blond") was correct, but
perhaps I had materialized as someone less impressive than
that conveyed. The idea of me often seemed to exceed the
reality.

Would I want to share my world with a woman who
might have expected the ideal?

Looking at her now, a woman with wine-colored hair and eyebrows raised demandingly, I imagined that I did.

I couldn't help but stare at Natasha. Her clothing was a clash of counterculture and renaissance. Hippie skirt and peasant top. Ruffled edges. Rings on every finger, gaudy rings of astrological symbols and Celtic crosses. Natasha's long red hair was separated into two pigtails with purple ribbons braided throughout. She noticed me eyeing her clothes and turned to show me her profile, instinctively, like a model. She knew I was a photographer, and perhaps assumed that I needed to see her at both angles.

I felt warped in time, dressed in my sensible oxford shirt and khaki clam diggers, like a golf caddy being interviewed by a Pre-Raphaelite flower child.

Natasha checked her watch, a gaudy marcasite piece with tiny cameos across the band. "Fuck her!" she said, referring to Valerie, our absent roommate.

"Maybe she was caught in traffic?" I took a deep sip of cappuccino, then yanked my mouth back from the drink, my tongue numb, flat with burn. As always, the barrista had steamed my milk too long.

Natasha rolled her eyes and fixed her gaze upon me. Across the table from her, I felt as though I had become the most important person in the world. "Listen. I know we are aliens at this point, but I think it's dangerous for a woman to travel alone." Her words had come out overly enunciated and slowed, as though she were speaking in a large, cavernous room, waiting around for the echoes. "And since we are spending so much goddamn money on our plane tickets, do you want to go over early with me, get rail passes, and see as much as we can?"

"Well, I hadn't considered that."

She paused to open the plastic lid on her cup and dump two small pouches of sugar into her iced tea. *"Sucre,"* she mumbled to herself, then looked up.

"I took three years of French. Do you speak it?"

"German." I'd already quickly decided not to mention that I also knew some French, since I believed what I knew was not enough to actually count. Besides, it felt as if she were forcing me into a decision I hadn't yet made.

Her lips puckered, pouting, and she cast her gaze to the floor, unimpressed. "Pouah!" Her braids flipped. "I don't plan to go to Germany. I mean, if you want to go, that's your prerogative. I'd just want to be where it's beautiful and romantic. My psychic says I'm going to meet my knight in shining armor this summer."

Natasha grinned at these words. She pulled her straw from her cup and pressed the end to her tongue. Suck, pinch, release. Her pink tongue stretched out. Watching her made me blush suddenly, and I looked away.

"Aren't photographers supposed to carry their cameras on them at all times?" she asked, and reached into her pocket to pull out a small book with a Chinese print cover. She theatrically ran her fingers across the delicate cloth material as if mesmerized by its aesthetics. "I always carry my journals. My best poems have been inspired by everyday things. Did I tell you I was published in *Muse Magazine*?"

I hadn't heard of *Muse Magazine,* so all I could do was shake my head. I was usually quiet, but I felt different with Natasha. I could have offered to share my portfolio with her, however, I felt stunned in her company, unable to speak. She seemed to be creating all the momentum, leaving me frozen in the wake of her spell. I even wondered if perhaps she could be one of those psychic vampires I had read about in articles and books, who, due to their own inability to generate energy, steal energy from others to achieve a kind of high.

"This poem was about a traffic light." She smiled philosophically, head tilted. "It was called 'Implications at an Intersection.'"

The phrase seemed to mirror my thoughts exactly. "I hadn't planned on traveling early," I mumbled, again avoiding her eyes.

"So why not have an adventure? Live a little."

Moments later she offered to loan me her copy of the Eurorail book that was in her car, and asked me to follow her out to the parking garage.

As soon as we left the café, Natasha lit a cigarette with such obvious pleasure I almost felt like I was infringing upon the moment. "What's that?" she asked, referring to the portfolio I was carrying.

"Just some photos."

"Oh, can I see?"

"Well, I haven't updated it lately and—"

"Hold my cigarette, will you?" she said, handing it to me and ignoring my refusal. She snatched the portfolio from my arms and unzipped it.

"Wow," she said, turning each page almost more slowly than I could bear. "You are really good. I almost feel I've seen some of these before. Have you been published?"

"No," I said, embarrassed. I'd heard this before, the comments about my having "a classic eye." What this meant to me was that my photos held somewhat of a derivative nature.

"Students and teachers generally like my work right away," I continued. "I think it's a dead sign of artistic failure."

"Yeah, you must not threaten anyone," Natasha said, stepping into her blue coupe and handing my portfolio back to me. My hand was shaking nervously, and I handed her back the cigarette I'd been reluctant to hold, which now had a long stem of gray ash hanging loosely. She smiled and tapped it, the ashes falling close to my sandals, then brought the cigarette to her lips.

"You will return from Europe as a force to be reckoned with," she said. "That is, if you let her work her magic."

Tori Amos's heavy piano chords blared from the speakers as Natasha drove away, cigarette smoke trailing from a crack in her tinted window. I took notice of her license plate: "Rescue Me."

Chapter 2

Armored Ghost

Meticulously vacuumed white carpet, a pale blue pillowcase stained with brown mascara, Beverly Hills lawns toasted to golden perfection from the unrelenting heat. I imagined Mother's house, fully aware that it could be my world this summer, had it not been for the Prague poetry program.

"You're going to travel fifteen days with a stranger?" Mother had asked, rolling her words around to make the idea seem foolish.

"We've decided to get the most for our money by seeing as much of the Continent as possible before heading to Prague."

I had called my mother from my bedroom phone, even though she was just downstairs. She hated it when I did this and repeatedly warned me that I was becoming lazy—which was true, but I saw no harm in it.

Mother grunted. "It's not your money."

"Yes, Mother," I said, turning up the volume of my stereo. "I know."

"I just don't see why you have to make this summer into such a production. Isn't being in the photography school enough?"

If my life was a production, then I was a member of the supporting cast, and the lead role was played by my mother. Although photography was my choice, I was reminded of the pitfalls of this choice every day and of the choices I hadn't made, the choices I could have made that might have provided me with a more prominent place in society.

"Who is this person, anyway? Do you even know this girl? Are you sure you can trust rooming with a stranger? What if she steals?"

"She's a poet, Mother. Poets only steal your soul."

Mother produced a great huff into the receiver and I pictured her rolling her eyes, to illustrate just how irrelevant she thought my opinion was.

I fell back onto my bed and opened a magazine. *Modern Photographer.* It was published in French. I could only read some parts of it, but that didn't matter, since I had bought it for the photos. I opened to a two-page spread on fetishism. The photo was of a pair of breasts dripping with chocolate.

"Hel-lo?" Mother said, using her singsong voice. "What if she distracts you from your studies and wants to do nothing but ditch class, and drink and smoke like all eastern Europeans? What kind of memories do you wish to make with this trip?"

I recalled Natasha lighting up as soon as we'd left the café, smoking as if it were another affectation, like her dress and her attraction to metaphors. She had inhaled the smoke slowly, allowing it to linger inside for a long time, filling all the corners of her mouth, her expression becoming nearly a smile before she finally exhaled.

"I mean it," Mother continued. "Your relationship with your professors is very important. You don't want to damage that."

"Please. You are so old-fashioned. Professors are the ones trying to make *us* take *them* seriously."

"Turn that music down. How can you hear me with that stuff blaring?"

"That's precisely the point," I hollered, hanging up. I slapped the magazine closed and stuffed my head into the swell of my pillows.

"Rescue me," I whispered.

On the plane I felt restless, trying to read a book Mother had bought me for the trip. I never enjoyed reading books I've been given. Something about reading another person's choice took away the chance of mystery and exclusivity I craved.

I noticed a woman looking at me from across the aisle. I avoided her gaze.

A flight attendant approached, carrying a tray full of tiny plastic cups of water. I took one and drank it down.

"Enjoying your read?" I heard a female voice ask.

I looked up and saw the woman across the aisle sipping her water and offering a polite smile. "I just live for Nora Collins," she began. "Does that woman understand the games that men and women play!"

I nodded.

"Actually, I haven't read *that* one," she said, pointing to my book, which was open, facedown, on the empty seat next to me, "But as soon as I can, I will. The airport bookstore was sold out."

"That's a shame," I said, my voice dripping with disinterest.

"Yes," she said, retreating.

I glanced down at the book, its front and back covers visible. On the front was a sketch of a beautiful dark-haired woman clinging to the shoulder of a hefty lumberjack-looking man.

The back featured a photo of the author, Nora Collins. She had long, fluffy dark hair, not unlike the heroine on the cover, but Nora was obviously overweight, probably living alone, smiling directly into the camera with nothing less than total confidence. Below this photo read the caption: "*Over Eighteen Months on the Best Seller List!*"

I grabbed the book again. It was heavy. I had only read the first twenty pages, but the thought of continuing seemed like a chore I couldn't bear to face; the plot was rife with manipulations and denial practiced by a woman who pretends not to want to submit to a man she has loved from afar all her life. Apparently, Mother believed that my tastes and pleasures ran synonymously with hers.

I closed the book and handed it to the woman. "Take it. You won't be disappointed, I'm sure."

"But you haven't finished it!" the woman said, her eyebrows narrowing as she set her empty cup down and reached out for the novel.

"Don't worry," I said. "I already know how it ends."

Chapter 3

Green Dragons

White walls and terra-cotta roofs. Clouds back-floating in blue sky.

Midday in Athens, after a fitful night trying to sleep on the plane and not succeeding. It was the first time I had been alone in a foreign country.

I used the telephone in the pension lobby, since I'd promised Mother I would call her as soon as I settled in Athens.

"Some drama with her ex apparently held Natasha up," I explained, reading the message the hotel desk clerk had handed me when I checked in. "She says she'll be here tomorrow."

"Well," Mother said. "She says that, but will she?"

The thought hadn't really occurred to me, and now that it had, I felt indifferent.

"What about the other one? The third roommate?"

"Valerie? She never made the effort to meet us, so we didn't invite her. Don't worry, I'll be fine."

"It feels like you've been gone so long," she said, then began relaying tidbits from the news that day, reminding me of things back home as though I might have forgotten.

She became quiet. "So, did you like the book I gave you?"
"Oh, yes," I lied.

"Wasn't the ending a surprise? I had no idea those two
would get back together," she said and sighed.

Annoyed, I crumpled the note from Natasha and tossed it
into a nearby wastebasket. I ran a hand through my hair and
let out a deep exhale. "I need to find a money exchange and
get some dinner."

"Well, do try to get two keys from the desk clerk if you
can, so you don't have to worry about the girl once she gets
there. She's been enough trouble."

Street vendors selling hot lamb souvlas basted in avgo-
lemono sauce. Vegetable bins overflowed with bright red,
juicy tomatoes. Wooden barrels displayed brown and purple
olives, nuts, and dried figs. An old woman with long gray hair
sat on a stool braiding garlic. Six-foot links of sausage hung
from the market rafters. Bleeding pigs' feet in plastic jars lined
indoor meat stands. The raw smells in the city market were
unlike any I had encountered in American markets—both
earthy and sweet.

Unusually famished, I filled up on the classics: Spanakopita
and Dolmades. Everywhere, pastry shops displayed brimming
trays of golden baklava—I devoured the flaky pastry, warm
honey dripping down my chin.

Later, walking around the Acropolis with its masses of
steps, alleys, and squares, I noticed people staring at me. I was
wearing a black sundress, a slight detour from the usual en-
sembles I put together, and wondered if the looks I was getting might have been due to my nationality. Even with a tan,
I stood out amongst all the olive complexions.

A young girl, probably about four years old and wearing a white lace dress, stopped at the outdoor restaurant tables, offering up her hat, which appeared to be full of coins. About an hour later I spotted the same girl standing on a corner, now with a larger group of beggars, totally transformed, barefoot, and banging a tambourine.

Citizens were aggressive about their meals in Athens. Café hosts stood in front of the Plaka square patios in starched white shirts, their sleeves rolled to the elbows, luring customers with flirtatious nods and smiles, pointing to empty chairs. Gypsy children ran barefoot through Dimarch Square, their feet filthy from the streets. I pulled out my camera and the children posed enthusiastically, then begged for money in return, which I gladly gave them. There was an old man riding a bicycle which was pulling about twelve feet of hay, and it seemed impossible. He had paused at an intersection, and I had just enough time to snap a shot with my camera. I usually didn't photograph people, not even candids, but this summer was already becoming an exception.

I heard beautiful Indian music coming from a jewelry shop and stopped in for a look. A man was engraving at a desk. Smells of musky incense swept the air of the room, pumping out from little silver holders and reminding me of the head shops I'd occasionally ventured into at home on Melrose. When the jeweler spotted me, he turned off the small machine and smiled, greeting me in English. Although not fluent, he spoke of interesting things, lighting up a cigarette which he rolled himself. He impressed me with his intellect, introducing me to the music he was playing, which turned out to be primitive Greek music backed by progressive percussions. Dimitris was in his early thirties, dark and tall, unlike Grant. I admired his profile when he looked down to write the name of the music onto a slip of paper for me.

"Why a woman so beautiful is out on her own?"

"I'm fine," I said. "I have a companion arriving tomorrow."

"Your husband?"

"A woman."

He smirked and seemed to have interpreted my answer differently than I'd intended.

"She's just a friend," I said.

The jewelry cases in his store displayed beautiful tooled earrings and bracelets. However, none were styles that I would wear, all of them much too elaborate for my simple wardrobe. Dimitris spotted me eyeing a ring with a strange Asian-looking cone in its center, and walked over and retrieved it from the case.

"Try this," he said. "I want to see it on you."

"That's okay. I'm just looking."

"To look well is to touch," he said, pulling the ring out from the velvet platform and taking my hand, forcing the ring on my middle finger.

I held it out in front of me, looking at it from different angles, observing how phallic the design was. I could feel my face blush, the heat traveling down into my neck and chest. I desperately needed a manicure, but hadn't realized it until now.

He grabbed my hand and took a closer look, examining both the ring and my nails. I finally laughed nervously, sliding my hand out from his grip.

"*Catastroph*—" he said, taking my hand once again, then observing my nails more closely. "You should take better care."

"I never wear jewelry," I said, pulling my hand back and trying to slip off the ring. My fingers had swelled from the salty foods and muggy air. I tugged, but the ring wouldn't budge.

"Let me," he said, and took my hand once more, placing my middle finger deep into his mouth. His hands and face were a golden olive color, and his hands smelled of tobacco. He slid his tongue around the area where the ring was, then set his teeth behind the metal and began to slowly tug, but the ring didn't move. His eyes were closed, which was good, because I was blushing even more now, wondering how he could stand to have my unkempt fingernails in his mouth.

Dimitris invited me up to his studio for a glass of ouzo, sliding down the garage-style doors of his shop and flipping a sign. His apartment was nothing more than a sex den; one room furnished with an unmade bed and a large sword hanging on the wall above the headboard. He handed me a glass and I tossed the thick, colorless liquid down my throat and felt it bleed warmth into my belly, minty and unsweet—it immediately lightened my head.

After bringing out a necklace that was lying on the kitchen counter and fastening it about my neck, he directed me toward a mirror, unzipping the top half of my sundress and pulling the black linen material down past my shoulders. My breasts were revealed as we both stood facing my reflection.

"See, beautiful," he said, taking his hand and fixing the necklace, straightening it in the center of my chest.

He pressed his mouth against my neck and his tongue slid into my ear like a prehensile tail, his whiskers scratching me.

It wasn't quite as exciting as the finger suck had been. I pulled back, a slight burning sensation lingering on my skin. We had only just begun, although I was already wishing it was over.

"You're not so shy with men," he whispered, turning me about to face him now, my hand involuntarily placed against the swell in his pants. "A blond panther."

I tore off Dimitris's pants as quickly as I had every other man's, telling myself that this experience would be unlike the rest, that Dimitris would understand me as no one ever had and that he would find secret ways to please me. But there was no more foreplay. The weight of his body on top of mine and the shocking sensation as he penetrated me made me think of sex with Grant, although not with any nostalgia.

I became lost in thought as I so often did during sex, looking around, observing the details of the room. Dimitris's room was nearly empty—nothing but bottles, a few discarded clothes, and the sword. The sheets smelled unlaundered and musky. I wondered how many lovers he had, and if the scent of the sheets revealed someone recently taken. My body remained tight, unable to loosen as Dimitris went to work.

He turned me over so that I was now on top of him and with each of his thrusts my body rocked, the heavy necklace knocking against my chest, further distracting me. I could see his ribs when he took in deep breaths and there was a scar— perhaps there had been a surgery. But it was not clear, as black hair concealed most of his chest. I considered, for a moment, what my future would be like if I fell in love with him—a man who lived on the other side of the world. A man who had heart problems. We would only be able to see each other on holidays and yet, this would make it all the more passionate.

Sirens came in from the streets, and I began to think of the gypsy child I had seen earlier, wondering if she was okay.

"Danielle, Danielle!" Dimitris whispered in his thick accent, so that my name came out more like "Daniellah."

He whispered Greek words into my ear and came quite unexpectedly, then rose to get a towel. I felt uninvolved in what had happened. Men seemed to respond more quickly to me when I was tensed up and tight—the exact opposite of what it took to get me off.

"Damn, you're good," he said.

His comment made me feel lonely, as though I had been rated. Unless it is the best experience one has ever had, one should not even attempt a comparative rating for lovemaking since it appoints the activity to be a talent, rather than an expression. Would it be fair to rate each other's expressions?

I dressed slowly and Dimitris watched, helping me zip up the back of my sundress and unlatching the necklace, sliding it off me, an instant release of weight. I took more pleasure in dressing in front of a man than I did undressing.

While I was buckling my sandals, Dimitris left the bed to fetch some water in the kitchen and while he was away, a mosquito began to buzz around me. As I rolled away from this irritation, I saw the long blade of the sword swing toward me, its silver blade shining. Dimitris set the sword on the mattress and stared at it. In a whispered voice, he said he envisioned the mosquito landing on the edge of the sword and bleeding to death.

"I've been reading of these things in a martial arts guide," Dimitris explained, his eyes on the sword with strict concentration. The buzzing stopped. "Next I will be going to Japan, to study and also get tattoos."

"What kind of tattoos?"

"All on my back and across—dragons. Dragons!" he said, rolling his "r"'s.

"You're fascinated with death."

"It's part of life."

I tried at the ring again, this time flattening my knuckle and pulling as hard as I could, harder than Dimitris had. It finally made it past my joints and freed itself to the floor, making a tinny sound and rolling across the wood. I picked it up from the dusty floor and placed it in Dimitris's hand, suddenly self-conscious that he might have taken this as a hint for him to give it to me to remember him by, or as some gesture of affection.

He tossed the ring on his bed and kissed me again, delicately this time, almost an apology. Everything we did seemed so mechanical, a prelude to the next predictable move. Warm air blew through his nostrils and against my face. Our last kiss— far too gentle to have been anything other than a good-bye.

I walked down the marble steps of his flat, feeling drained and noticing an attractive woman standing alone outside the door of Dimitris's shop, carrying a bottle of wine, waiting for him to reopen. She looked American.

Although the timing had been okay for me, I should have used a condom.

Walking back through the town square, back to my pension, I stopped at a corner mart and bought a magazine, some bottled water, and some deodorant packaged in a funky blue-green tube. Near the cash register was a bouquet of fresh pink carnations. I could smell their perfume, strong and sweet. The clerk pointed to them and began speaking in Greek, asking if I would like to buy the flowers. I shook my head gently, turning my attention away and handing him my coins for the magazine.

As I crossed Santagma Square, a gypsy boy began to harass me for some money. His eyes looked like the eyes of a tired dog. I tried to wave him away, shaking my head, but he wouldn't leave me alone, following me as I walked, pointing to his stomach. I had some dried fruit in my purse which I offered to him, but he wouldn't acknowledge the gesture. He got closer and I finally pushed him away, surprised by my physical hostility.

Back in the pension, I took a lukewarm shower. The toilet was a porcelain wading pool, more or less, with two places intended to separate my feet and keep them out of my urine, a small drain in the center. A weak light bulb flickered above my head. The sink was back in the bedroom.

The bed was too soft, with springs poking out of the mattress. The other bed, which was to be Natasha's, was just as saggy and abrasive. What I had considered necessities back home—hot water, the flushing of a toilet, paper towels, and soap—had suddenly become luxuries to me. I tossed and turned all night.

Without sleep, I start to die a little, I think.

When Natasha arrived the next afternoon, I was momentarily relieved. Coming down the airport escalators towards the baggage carousel, she was prettier than I'd remembered, and welcomed me with a bright smile.

"Hey, Camera Girl." She set down a large handbag and

looked around. I recognized the scent of faint perfume and tobacco about her. She immediately lit a cigarette and took a deep drag.

"Life is perfect." She exhaled. "I love being able to smoke at an airport."

Quickly, however, her eyes changed—she began to stare at me in that interrogating way as at our first meeting, and I experienced a reversal: a sudden desire to be alone again. Her suitcase finally came and I awkwardly followed her out of the airport, consciously trying not to judge her for having packed so inefficiently—she seemed to have brought a lot to be carrying throughout multiple cities.

"I want to remember this moment always. My first time abroad," Natasha said, outstretching her arms in the heavy air. We were waiting for a taxi, in the midst of a bustling station. Frequent puffs of stale bus fumes choked out of exhaust pipes and horns blew like mad alarms.

Her breasts were pressed tight across the front of her linen blouse, producing a mass of wrinkles below them. Most likely she had slept in the shirt.

Natasha's complexion appeared healthy and well-rested, her features as relaxed as a child's. My own flight over had been miserable, as I'd spent the last half of it chewing down the end of a pencil and fidgeting with the air conditioner dial above my seat.

I pulled out my map of the city, eager to get on with our journey.

Natasha, it seemed, had her own agenda.

"Take my picture," she demanded.

I was wearing my camera across my chest and I suddenly realized what an open invitation it must have been. Again, I wished I were alone.

"I left my camera on my bed back home," Natasha confessed, taking another long drag. "I realized it on the air-
plane."

I folded the map back up, sliding it into my jeans pocket.
Taxis whizzed by us, not bothering to stop. Natasha stood
posed, waiting for me to take her "snapshot." Irritated, I reflected that it was a type of photography I despised shooting—
something over and done with too quickly, a waste of good
film and technique that offered nothing other than a moment's flattery. I strove for photographs that would survive.

Fingering my camera to make certain that the lens cap
was still on tight, making sure that all the pieces were still
there, I noticed how my hands trembled.

"So, you'll buy a little point-and-shoot here, I suppose?"
My voice took on the assuming air I'd intended as I pulled off
the lens cap and set it securely in my pocket. I was resenting
the implied obligation. This trip was meant to be a vacation
from such duties. How would I find time for myself if all my
attention was wrapped up in meeting her needs?

As I raised the camera to focus on her, Natasha brought
her hands to her hips, forcing a smile. And at that moment she
was possibly the most beautiful woman I had ever seen. She
wasn't a streamlined model, or modern-looking or even daring, but she had a complex face, some of her features like that
of a girl's, and others that seemed to be those of someone
older and wiser than her nineteen years could have afforded.
She had a wide mouth, expressive and innocent. Lips that
made me want to watch for subtle changes in their direction,
taking note of what might please her. I wanted to look longer
at her classic nose that swooped down gracefully and then
dipped back to form a little boot, lending her an air of rakish
sophistication. I wanted to gaze at those cat eyes that seemed

almost drugged and hypnotized. What kind of state, what type of hidden thoughts, would produce a pair of such luxurious windows? All these curiosities led me quickly back into a hypersensitive awareness. I was staring. But as a photographer about to take a picture, I couldn't escape. I was suddenly glad for the job she had appointed me for the trip, as it provided a sort of cover so as not to give my true feelings away: a woman was exciting me.

"And why should I buy a camera when I can depend on the kindness of my travel companion?" Natasha finally asked.

I relented.

Peering though the viewfinder, I noticed that her eyes were closed, her head tilted up into the sunshine, letting the heat caress her face. She brought her hands up in the air, extended her arms out wildly, her fingers spreading like wings. "Mmm," she said, stretching and taking in a deep breath. "I can smell my fate."

I pressed the shutter and all went dark.

I had never felt so uncomfortable in the company of another woman as I did on this trip. I recalled Nietzsche's words, "If you want to attract someone, act terribly embarrassed by his or her presence." If only Natasha were a man, I thought, then I'd really have something here.

Nights became my only refuge, where I allowed the darkness to envelop me. In our shadowy room which hid and protected my body from Natasha's sight, I silently caressed myself beneath the covers of my small bed, riding off the toil of our days together and thrilling at my trivial moment of escape. My fingers sliding deep into the walls of my moistness, I tried to keep my breathing as silent and unchanging as possible, careful not to wake my travel companion. As long as

Natasha's breathing didn't change, her soft breaths that came and went like a low, evening tide, I felt safe, and took the moment to bring myself to climax—the only thing that seemed to relax me enough for sleep. Although touching myself in the company of a stranger, let alone a woman, was unlike anything I'd ever done, I demanded this singular act of pleasure as part of my daily agenda which was otherwise thwarted by Natasha's presence.

I would not allow her to damage my summer.

Beneath the now rich scented sheets, I writhed and sweated and finally dropped to the mattress, my legs buzzing beneath me. Overtired, my lids closed and I finally slept.

We never made it to the Greek islands, which Mother claimed were the only places worth visiting in Greece. We had eleven days to get to Prague, and visiting the islands would have taken up at least three of them. In an effort to keep things inexpensive enough to fit Natasha's limited budget, we avoided museum fees and tolls and spent our days lurking around Athens along with the mangy stray cats and dogs of the city. I tried to avoid capturing them in photos, working around their gray bodies that seemed to appear everywhere—filthy and confused. All the while, Natasha kept pleading, annoyed, in her almost habitual baby-talk "Get the kitty in the shot!" or "Now. Purdy please! You have to be quick to get the puppy, too!" I wasn't the best travel companion for Natasha, and she already seemed bored with me. She walked ahead of me, flitting from place to place, uninterested in what I might have wanted to see or do, probably scouting for her "knight in shining armor." I watched the back of her head as she walked, her hair trailing down her back, longer in the center than it was on the sides, like a young girl's.

Natasha gave up on ideas quickly, making snap judgments at mere appearances. If the outside of a gallery or restaurant appeared simple or dim, Natasha would wrinkle up her face and look around, hoping something better might be around the corner. With time, I began to notice how she was attracted to things a teenage traveler would be drawn to: retro American diners, bright, colorful buildings that were highly commercialized, with disco music thumping—signposts that promised happiness. Had she come all the way for this?

I tagged along to the Hard Rock Café and Planet Hollywood. Waitresses stood on top of our tables, sneakers and all, and performed choreographed dances to songs like "YMCA" and the "Macarena," leading the room full of customers through the routine. Natasha stood on the booth seat and followed along. She was a great sport, but I could see her blushing as she went through the motions—perhaps aware that all eyes, especially male eyes, were on her. She was wearing a white lace blouse with puffy sleeves that buttoned up the front with tiny rhinestones, the top few buttons undone, baring a mass of cleavage. Her large breasts jounced along to each movement, like a cheerleader's. She coaxed me to participate, tugging on me and trying to pull me from my seated position. As kind as her efforts were to include me, I refused to participate. I had a problem with music that sounded that happy. I refused to belong to the school of the naïve, which often flocked to things overly idyllic.

I was reminded of a girl who had graduated from high school with me and, wanting to experience what it felt like to be a "real princess," went off to work at Disney's Magic Kingdom, the "happiest place on earth," only to discover that employees were frying themselves on drugs to keep up the smiles.

I had signed up for this summer as an escape from mediocrity, and here I was, burying myself in it for Natasha's companionship. At this rate, my plans for making headway with my art in Prague would be shot.

At dinner our first night together I used silverware, while Natasha ate with her fingers. As we mindlessly inhaled our "Oriental" chicken salads, I was glad to have had yesterday to myself, choosing where I ate. I had silently craved a Greek pizza topped with fish and feta cheese and olives and served on a cracker-like crust, which I'd caught sight of along one of those cafés with outdoor seating.

I was forced to raise my voice over the music as I spoke to her across the table about old movies I liked, mentioning Claudette Colbert, Bette Davis, and Shirley MacLaine. How the standards for beauty were different in the past, that actresses didn't have to be slaves to box office draws, since their success wasn't gauged solely upon the shape of their bodies. I suggested that being a successful actress back in the early days of Hollywood seemed to require more originality, something I preferred. Natasha responded to these comments with disinterest, licking her fingers, saying that she wasn't familiar with old films since they were in black and white. She explained how "the now" was most important to her, and that I should consider studying Zen Buddhism.

"How can you not like black-and-white films?"

"They look so boring," she said. "All of them, they seem so dull."

Just when I thought there was no chance that I would ever fall in like with Natasha, she got up and came around to my side of the booth and sidled up to me, shoulder to shoulder. "I have an idea."

"Wait, how do you do that?" I asked, trying to raise one of my eyebrows the way she did.

Ironically, Natasha had a face that might have made the big screen back in the days. Her beauty seemed original enough to elicit vintage stardom, if only a stardom that I was privy to.

"I don't know," she said. "I think it's natural. You just can or you can't."

I kept trying, eventually needing to clamp my fingers to keep one brow down while I raised the other.

"There," I said proudly at my imitation. "Do I look mysterious?"

Natasha let out a loud burst of laughter. "You are so funny."

Her next words were quiet. "I want to kiss someone."

The words came out slowly and clearly, aimed right in my direction.

"I want to kiss someone in Greece," she repeated.

Did she want to kiss me? She was sitting so close to me now, I felt nervous.

She dropped her brow and lowered her head. "Those guys over there are cute." Her eyes darted off to the side and I turned my head.

"Don't look yet!"

"I already noticed them," I said. "They came in right after we did and have been staring at us the whole time. They're out prowling tonight."

I intended this comment to be an insult.

"Well," she said, making a purring sound with her tongue, "so am I."

She turned and looked over at them and one of the boys smiled back at her, tipping his hat. Both were attractive in a young and common way—in a way that most city boys are, dressed stylishly with baseball hats and tiny gold earrings, heads perpetually swiveling, as if they had lost some part of their youth.

"Greek men are terrible in bed," I said.

She looked back at me as though I were someone else, then smiled.

"I would never just get into a car with two strange boys and let them take me where they wanted," I said to Natasha as we stood outside the restaurant, waiting for the car. It would be dark soon, but the air was still warm enough that we didn't need to wear sweaters—the evening sun still looming in the horizon, warming my cheeks and arms.

"But we're in Europe," she said, "and that changes everything. We need to get out of our skins for a while. Let's take some risks we wouldn't take at home. Besides, they say they have a Jeep."

I wasn't convinced.

"You had your Greek, Danielle, now it's my turn."

We sat in the backseat of a red Suzuki Samurai, holding our hair to keep it from blowing into our eyes, while the boys sat up front, singing at the top of their lungs to top forty American music, their accents momentarily gone. Thanos, the driver, seemed to be speeding too fast for such narrow streets. He had said the lookout spot was just ten minutes away, and I could now see that measuring distance by time rather than miles was to their advantage. Thanos and his friend, Jorge, seemed happy, and picking up two American girls must have had something to do with it. Maybe also the fact that they believed the Suzuki they owned was an actual Jeep.

The cheap red car twisted up a rough dirt road, the air

cooling as we rose in elevation. Finally, Thanos hit the brakes and the car stopped at the top of a small mountain. The engine shook and died.

"Here we are, ladies," said Thanos. "The most romantic view in all of Athens."

There was a sign, written in both Greek and English. It read "No camping, hunting, fires, or horn blowing."

"What is there to hunt up here?" Natasha asked.

The boys exchanged a few words in Greek and chuckled. "I think you call them bunnies," Thanos said.

We parked and Thanos came around to our door, giving Natasha his hand. I watched her look at him, placing her palm in his. "Oh, it's so beautiful," she said, stepping out.

"Yes," Thanos agreed, taking off his hat, revealing a full head of dark brown curls.

The air was cold and light now and smelled of high altitudes, of dust and of sea. The sun was falling fast. The air whipped through my clothes as I stood near the edge of the cliff, overlooking all of Athens. We'd arrived just in time for a blood orange sunset, the buildings glowing below in a haze of color and smog. From the height, we looked down at the city enclosed by high hills, and behind them, suburbs extended out as far as the eye could see, and beyond that, the ocean. In the labyrinth of the city, small white houses with blue trim ascended the hillsides, clotheslines linking them together like string, and in the center of all this were the famous monuments which seemed to have been swallowed by the greater whole.

I didn't need the view or the company tonight. I had seen enough spectacular sights for one day.

"All cities look the same," I said, peering out at a mass of jammed up structures, a view that resembled the view from Los Angeles's Getty Museum—hill after hill of sprawling apartment complexes, suburbs, and industrial factories. A concrete jungle. At least there was no admission charge for this view, although I'd come a long way from home to see it. "Looks just like L.A. to me."

Jorge must have sensed my disappointment and opened his jacket to me, revealing a black leather flask. He pointed to a bench nearby. He couldn't speak any English aside from the American songs he sang along to, and for that I was glad. I didn't feel like talking.

We sat on the bench and took turns sipping from his flask, while Natasha and her Romeo sat in the grass, overlooking the city. It was excessively windy and I wrapped my arms around my shoulders, shivering, feeling the goose bumps rise on my skin. Jorge began to slide closer and closer to me, until finally he took off his coat and offered it to me. I shook my head no. When I glanced back at Natasha, I could see she was now wearing Thanos's jacket. I wondered if that was what had prompted my mute escort to have made the gesture, if he couldn't think up anything original.

While we were riding in the backseat, I had decided that Jorge was better looking than Natasha's date, and that he had nice eyes, but now that he was next to me, I avoided them. I refrained from finishing off the flask that he passed to me—it was the least I could do for him, since he wasn't going to get a kiss out of me. Something about their elementary theatrics—parking on a hill as though a pretty view was some sort of prelude to a kiss or a ticket to my heart—the whole scene made me weary, and strangely protective of Natasha. Finally, Jorge made a lunge toward me and I got up and skipped over to the wanna-be Jeep.

The sun had practically set and there was an approaching cloud bank. It had seemed like the sun would never disappear into the horizon, but finally it had.

"You guys ready?" I shouted over to Natasha and Thanos. They were still seated on the grass, facing each other, his hand playfully touching her knee. She was giggling. I couldn't tell if she had gotten her kiss yet.

Her laughter demanded my attention, her bright vibrations that multiplied like a bouncing ball. She lay back on the blanket as the stranger tickled her beneath her arms, near her chest, in the cave of her neck, and along her sides. She began to howl, trying to push him off of her, but to no success. He had her pinned and was not going to let her go, so long as he continued to bring her bliss.

I watched and waited for the kiss she was after, but it hadn't come, not to my knowledge anyhow. Surprisingly, however, other intimations took place. He took his jacket off her shoulders and began to unbutton her blouse. I felt self-conscious just standing there, watching, so I slipped back over to where Jorge was sitting, taking his coat from him, while remaining watchful of Natasha.

With the heavy leather jacket now covering my shoulders, I looked back at Natasha who was now helping the stranger remove her bra. Unbeknownst to him, it unsnapped in the front. Her weighty breasts fell from the satin cups and, strangely, I felt a surge of excitement pass through my body.

Natasha stretched out her arms and smiled at the man, taking in a deep breath. He began to kiss her nipples and before another moment passed, she pushed him away, got to her feet and ran over to the edge of the cliff. For a moment I did not breathe, watching Natasha peer out over the edge. I wondered what her intentions were, and anticipated, for some reason, disaster, although the expression on her face appeared peaceful. I wondered why she had taken off her top, and then concluded that her true Greek fantasy must have involved more than just a kiss. She spread her arms out and screamed a pleasurable cry to the city, then turned back to her lover.

He could see that she was thrilled by the liberty she was experiencing, and took advantage of her mood, motioning to her to take off her pants.

My face flushed as I watched her coax her friend into removing his pants first. Slowly, she followed his lead, and they both became naked.

His penis was thin but long, his erection rising up towards his navel. Her pubic hair was light brown, unlike the wine red hair on her head. The man reached down and petted between Natasha's legs and, after letting out a gasp, Natasha grabbed her date by the waist and leaned back so that the man could slide himself into her.

For a solid five minutes the two had sex right before Jorge and me, although each time I felt their eyes turning towards us, I would quickly turn to Jorge, leaning closer to him, pretending to be preoccupied with him.

But neither he nor I exchanged a word. I had nothing to say to him and felt a queer mix of both desire and fury. Each time the man pressed himself into Natasha or pawed at her breasts I questioned the laws of the universe, wondering what had allowed this union to happen. All he had had to do was show up.

For a brief moment, I wished I were him.

Although my body had become warm, I did not remove the jacket that was still about my shoulders. I was pretending to have accepted Jorge's hospitality, only to have the excuse of hiding beneath the coat.

Natasha's moaning was melodious and sexy, and everything I could imagine a man would want to hear, although I sensed a slight affectation. Nevertheless, my insides stirred as I imagined how it might feel to be in his place, and what he could have done differently to discover a more authentic cry of pleasure from Natasha.

My panties became wet between my thighs, my mind thick with envy. I slid my hand up along the front of my shirt, across one of my breasts, and through the cotton and my bra I was able to feel that the tips of my nipples were hard.

Mutual sighs echoed and when I took one last look at the couple, they were no longer standing naked at the cliff, but had made it back to the car blanket. She was lying on her stomach, and he was finishing himself on her backside. Her head flipped from side to side as she squirmed below his blows of what I imagined to be hot and soothing.

I wondered if she had gotten what she wanted and then suddenly felt a wave of shame.

Looking back to Jorge, I could see he was no longer interested in me. I felt disgusted with myself before him, and avoided eye contact at all costs, slipped off his jacket, and offered it back to him. He drew it back sharply, throwing it over a shoulder and turning away from me.

So artlessly I had spied. And yet, a part of me harbored no regret. Jorge meant nothing to me, and so long as we never saw either man again, Natasha would never know the extent of my curiosity.

I was cold again and the wind was blowing my hair around. I felt abandoned, ironically wishing I had the generic routine of our travels back.

Moments later Natasha stood, redressed, and handing Thanos's jacket back to him with a grin.

"*Merci,*" she said, perhaps thinking that a Greek would understand French better than "thank you."

Natasha had me take a photo of her and Thanos, smiling next to the edge of the cliff. I didn't bother asking for her to take a shot of me with Jorge.

We all went back to the car, where Jorge was waiting, leaning against one of the back doors, looking cynical. I felt his eyes on me, as well as the others' eyes on me and my face flushed at the thought of Natasha having found me out. Yet when she eyed my body up and down, I could see that she was simply searching for signs that I, too, had enjoyed myself. The heat of my cheeks must have convinced her that I had.

"You look like you've been naughty," she said, and winked.

The heat burned into me the more. "I should have brought a jacket," I said.

I opened the door of the car and charged into the back. Natasha sat in the front passenger seat, so that she was no longer next to me, and was next to Thanos. Jorge slid in next to me and turned his hat down. "Go!" he said awkwardly to Thanos—his first spoken word in English.

Other than having missed a notch on one of her shirt buttons, nothing else about Natasha appeared changed or even disheveled. Her long hair lay neatly down her back. Her make-up—untouched, unsmeared. Her eyes—bright and curious as though she'd seen nothing more unusual than an exceptional lookout view. It was almost as if nothing had happened, and for a brief moment, I wondered if the whole affair had been imagined.

Natasha was smart enough not to have Thanos drop us at our pension. If he had, we might have continued to hear from him for the rest of our stay in Greece. Instead, she sweetly directed him to a more upscale hotel three blocks from where we were staying, and before letting me out of the backseat, Natasha leaned over and looked Thanos straight in the eyes.

"What about my kiss?" she asked, coyly biting her bottom lip, eyebrows raised inquisitively.

And then he gave her the kiss she'd been waiting for all night.

I'll never forget the sound of wetness as they kissed. It was awkward—I was trapped in the backseat with nothing to do but watch. I didn't dare look over at Jorge next to me, probably wondering why he had been so unlucky as to have gotten stuck with me.

Finally, Natasha pulled back and smiled at Thanos.

"I won't forget this," she said, grabbing her purse and climbing out of the car.

As I stepped out, I heard Thanos's voice call, "Wait." When I looked back in I realized he was talking to me.

"Nest time take a picture. It will last longer."

Both men laughed, Jorge especially, and I pretended not to have heard the insult, slamming the door quickly and skipping to catch up with Natasha.

The Suzuki sped away, the engine sounding as rough and impatient as the two men had been, and Natasha turned and waved dreamily back at them, as though saying good-bye to an adoring audience. She still had the warm smirk on her face and I looked quickly away from her, out at the littered street. A shabby gray cat ran past us and meowed, but Natasha was so lost in thought she didn't even notice.

Vouliagmeni beach, just outside of Athens. A bleak view. Cold, gray rocks beneath our slipping feet. Smell of fish and potatoes frying nearby. A vista of vague, muddy outcroppings punctuated by slivers of dark sand. Sun worshippers dotting the beach, hoping to catch at least the ultraviolet rays. Outdoor showers adorned with littered clothing appearing weather-beaten and trashed. Everywhere, dark, oiled men roasting atop foil liners and saggy, topless women bending to retrieve shells. Local men followed behind us, making clicking sounds as if we were small animals. "Tsch-tsch."

Natasha flipped the men off. "Maybe I'll go topless," she said, looking over at me. "Make them really eat their hearts out."

I laughed, hoping that she was kidding.

Old men were clad in bright-colored Speedos. Our eyes couldn't help but land on the myriad fluorescent crotches.

"I hate it when it's all smashed into a package like that," Natasha said too loudly.

"Maybe we'll find an art gallery nearby," I said, ignoring her comment and wishing we could leave the beach. But before I could turn away, Natasha approached one of the older men near the water fountain, one who was wearing leaf-green polyester bikini bottoms that emphasized his wrinkled brown thighs.

Natasha gestured to the old man, and then pointed to the camera dangling from my neck, which felt heavier than ever. The old man smiled. They drew closer, putting their arms around each other, obviously waiting for me to take the picture.

A gust of hot wind blew my sun hat off and the white afternoon sun washed across my eyes, almost blinding me.

I took the picture.

Natasha gave the old man a peck on the cheek and squealed with satisfaction as we walked off, throwing an arm around my shoulder.

"You absolutely *have* to make doubles," she said, giggling. She held her angular features high, obviously pleased with herself. I felt her eyes shift over to me for my approval. "I should have taken off my top, huh?"

I pushed her arm away, feeling warm.

"Oh, come on," she said. "Lighten up. We probably just made that old pervert's day."

I trudged ahead, approaching a garish section of town with high-end boutiques, featuring women emerging from stores dressed in clothes that cost more than my tuition last semester and carrying bright shopping bags.

I couldn't hold my feelings in anymore. I wanted to hear them hit the air with a bang: "This was exactly what my mother had warned me of—wasting my stay abroad."

"Consider the shot mine, then."

As I stomped ahead, I began to cook up images of Natasha wandering the hot beach alone with her breasts exposed had I not been there with her. "I suppose I'm ruining your vacation, keeping you from living," I hollered back.

Natasha came up close behind me and tickled me around the underside of my arms. "I'd never give you that power."

"Don't," I said, stopping on the sidewalk. My camera swung heavily on my neck, then hit my chest. I set my bag down and pulled the camera off my neck, placing it in the bag and zipping it tight. "Photography is a privilege not to be taken advantage of. It's obvious what you wanted out of that: a snapshot that you can hang on your refrigerator and laugh at."

"Maybe. Or maybe it might have turned out kind of artsy."

"Something to add to my professional portfolio?" I asked, readjusting the straps on my camera bag, double-checking inside to make sure that the lens cap was on. I hated that word "artsy"—a term used when people couldn't make up their minds about something.

We were standing in front of a fancy dress shop with garish red dresses displayed in the window, long slits running up each leg. The faces on the mannequins seemed expressive, almost judging. They had pendulous breasts, embarrassingly large for dummies. The manufacturer had taken obvious pleasures in his or her creations, beyond the simple purpose of displaying clothes. Mannequins like these didn't exist in America. I had to walk away from them.

"Did you start your period?" she asked, following me. "Because I have hard ones, too, and I mean *hard*. Bad moods. Heavy bleeding and cramps. Hunger, and I mean *hunger*! Are you hungry?"

"No," I said. "I'm not hungry or bleeding. I'm just . . . different from you. And I'm worried about this trip. I feel we don't get along."

"Well, I do what I please, so get used to it. Show me a famous artist who isn't difficult. When it comes to art you have to take risks."

"But *offensive*?"

"We all have our own perspectives."

The pungent odor of shellfish from a nearby restaurant filled my lungs and I brought my hand to cover my nose and mouth, trying not to breathe in the odor.

"That seems selfish," I said, my voice muffled.

A look of calm suddenly washed over Natasha's face. "Someday you may learn that there is nothing wrong with being selfish sometimes."

She spun on her heel and walked away.

Within moments she was out of sight, heading in the opposite direction of the bus line. She'd made her point by leaving me there, by myself. I continued walking the same direction we had come, burning anger for every word she had said and at the same time, wondering if she would be able to find her way back.

* * *

The air seemed thicker than it had earlier, the afternoon sun now setting. I had to wrap my sweater around my waist to cool off. Later on, I didn't see her on the bus and she wasn't back at our room. I wondered how she would get home, since I knew she couldn't afford the taxi fare for that distance. Hours passed and I sat in the room, flipping through a Greek magazine, wondering where she was. The magazine was filled with photographs of European landscapes. Usually, I would have carefully studied the photos I was looking at, the centuries-old architecture in muted pastel colors, superior framing and alignment of shadow and light. Normally, I would be curious about what type of film had been used, the speed and settings necessary to produce a given shot. But tonight the magazine was nothing more than a way to pass the time. Art was a distraction when Natasha wasn't there and my sudden loneliness contradicted my ethics: I sought pictures as a means to abandon thinking.

But it didn't work. I kept thinking back to the beach, how interesting it would have been to just stroll the shore, surreptitiously checking out the locals, a Greek version of people-watching. I did the same thing back at school, unobtrusively, of course, often in libraries or hallways. But the bodies in Greece were unclothed. Some of the bodies might have even been attractive. I could have given myself this experience had I only been more flexible. I should have just stayed on at Vougliamani, finishing our evening together, despite our differences. My regret was overwhelming.

I took a long shower, washing the sun and salt from my skin, and slipped on clean pajamas.

Natasha returned well past dark. She looked extremely disheveled, her hair in knots and her skin flushed pink, her shirt now untucked and wrinkled about her curves. It was near midnight.

"Where have you been? I was worried."

She pulled her bra and panties out from her pocket and lay them across a chair. "I went to an orgy in the back of a *taverna*—something to write home about."

Lying in the small single bed, my long legs stretched out almost over the edge, I closed the journal I'd been writing in and turned back to face Natasha's bed. It was too hot for me to be wearing pajamas, but I was not as brave as Natasha, flaunting her pale curves in a loose night slip, her breasts and thighs blooming out from the edges. I wondered if what she had said about the orgy had been true, or if she was just saying it to get a rise out of me. I looked down at my own body, petite breasts, flat tummy, and trim thighs, clad in light cotton kimono pants and matching top, wishing something in me would flower or ripen.

"An artist's model," my mother would often say about my body—which I found more insulting than complimentary as it so confined my vision of "art."

Natasha appeared to be exhausted. Her eyes were still open. She was lying on her back, facing the ceiling. My camera bag lay just below her bed, its crisp, clean red canvas, the safe, double straps. I hated looking at it now.

"You know Annie Leibovitz?" I asked.

"Of course," Natasha answered, not bothering to turn to me. "She became famous with that photograph of John and Yoko in a hug, taken right before he was killed."

Natasha continued. "My mother and I play Lennon records together sometimes. I miss her. She must be at work right now."

Natasha sat up in bed and reached for her cigarettes and matches, her muscular legs and buttocks flexing like a dancer's.

Red wavy strands fell onto her shoulders, collarbone, and chest. Her eyes had grown a paler green, and I wondered if she might have been crying earlier. I felt the urge again to touch her. Her skin looked ivory smooth. I wondered what it might be like to massage her, what her skin smelled like.

She threw the pack of cigarettes down. It was empty.

"Leibovitz holds a transcendental belief that beauty and truth await discovery in familiar intimate surroundings. What do you think of that?"

She paused, looking confused.

"Leibovitz," I repeated. "Do you agree with her that beauty is best found in the simple things around you?"

"Familiar doesn't always mean simple." She stood up and went for her shoes and sweater, her face pinched.

Natasha let out a long exhale. "Honestly, if I were you," she said, "I wouldn't worry if Annie Leibovitz knows her shit or not. She's obviously got it." Natasha lifted her chin toward me, some sort of see-you-later gesture, before leaving the room. "And *you* don't. You're too afraid."

The door slammed.

She was right. I owned dozens of photo books spanning decades of work from numerous photographers. I attended nearly every exhibit that came to Los Angeles. I bought art and hung it on my walls. Still, I couldn't get it. I was a decent photographer, my work crisp and detailed, but I was afraid of portraits. She'd seen my work and she knew how I kept my field of view safely focused on California architecture and landscapes. Knotty pines. Modern houses.

In the university department, classmates and professors flipped through my portfolio with a look of genuine approval until about halfway through, the question would inevitably come: "Hey? How come there aren't any people in these?"

My answer was always diluted; I would make reference to trying to retain a theme for my portfolio, or I'd say that these were simply the shots which people preferred from my collection. Never once had I confessed the truth—that shooting people made me uncomfortable and that I didn't like to look others in the eye. Facing this now, I began to doubt myself as a photographer. How could a woman such as I, who avoided confrontation, ever have authority as an artist?

Maybe I really *was* wasting Mother's money.

Natasha made up quickly with me by hating Dimitris. I brought her to his jewelry store and introduced them, whispering to Natasha that he had been a lousy lay—something I had never said about anyone. It was as though Natasha's previous disappointment in me had been supplanted with someone more convenient to discard. She took his business card from his long fingers and read it with mocking contempt, her voice guttural and clipped: "Greek arts and leather stuff by Dimitris."

He watched patiently as Natasha browsed through the handcrafted sterling ring collections and braided belts as though there was supposed to be something there for her. He pointed to her eyes and smiled. "Beautiful," he said.

Unimpressed, she asked to get a closer look at several items, making Dimitris unlock almost every glass case and take out each satin-covered ring platform so she could try them on. He followed the orders quietly, nearly apologetic. I had a difficult time believing I had ever slept with him. Natasha purchased nothing.

After we left the store, Natasha said I had strange taste in men.

"And I thought you said you were picky!"

We walked down the narrow streets that allowed only foot traffic, passing stone churches, meandering through numerous shops.

Cutting through the National Gardens was a way to escape the noise and heat of the city. Beneath the trees we wandered, chasing ducks, observing tropical plants, and resting on park benches. The air smelled wet and green. We bought birdseed and fed the doves which flocked around us, landing on our bodies, bravely perching on our arms and backs and heads. If Mother had seen this she would have thrown a fit about how filthy birds are, how they carry diseases and how I could have gotten staph. I finally shooed them off my body, while Natasha allowed them to linger.

"I would never date a man who was thin and hairy," she said, emptying the last of the seed on the ground while trying, at the same time, not to disturb the birds that were perched on her shoulders. "Not even if he gave me a discount."

"Do you prefer men who are fat and bald?"

"Dimitris has kind eyes, but you could do better. Take a picture of me."

Back in the Plaka, Natasha ran her fingers along the fabrics that were displayed out on the walkway, light cotton and gauze fibers in bold colors: blue, white, and yellow. She looked everyone in the eyes as we passed them.

Cafés with striped awnings and bright white umbrellas lined the streets. Two handsome hosts were able to lure Natasha into trying some Greek cuisine, something I had not been able to do since she had arrived.

We sat at an outdoor patio table at Byzantino and ordered eggplant salad, roasted potatoes, and scampi, and washed it

down with a white wine and bread dipped in olive oil. I fed
my leftovers to a dog that had wandered over to our table.
The young hosts called the dog Micho and, unlike the other
pups and cats they shooed away, they allowed Micho to
linger. After his meal, Micho sat at my feet beneath the table,
quietly resting his head against my shoe.

"Tell me about the other night," I said. "At the *taverna*."

"Oh, my God." Natasha laughed. "You believed me?"

"Why wouldn't I?"

There was a pause. "I went swimming."

Two girls came by our table selling flowers, interrupting
our conversation. One of them was about sixteen years old,
and very beautiful in the classic Greek way, long black hair
falling to her waist and shiny black eyes. She winked at me
and whispered to the younger girl who was with her. The girl
said in broken English, "My sister like you."

The older girl sent her younger sister away, and one of the
hosts came over to our table. The girl spoke to him quickly,
and he smiled, turning back to Natasha and me.

"She says that if you like, you can take her back to your
hotel for one hundred dollars and have your way, all night
long. Anything you want. Both of you."

"Have our way?" Natasha asked, glaring at the girl and
the host with disbelief.

I had an image, just then, of Natasha and I undressing this
girl, piece by piece, to find a body much more like an older
girl's, than that belonging to a young woman. Dutifully, the girl
would take her hair, long and thin as a filly's, and pull it back
away from her face, her bright copper eyes scanning ours for
feedback, preparing to please us in whatever ways we wished.
In her pubic region and beneath her arms, her hair would be
so thin that we would see it had only been there a few months

and lacked the thickness of women our age. But, despite her inexperience, she would be our sexual guide, validating our rights to soft pleasure and embracing a night involving only female lusts—be they secret.

"Would she like to just meet us at a club tonight and listen to some music instead?" Natasha asked the host. "We'll buy her drinks." She looked back at the girl and smiled politely.

The host exchanged more words with the girl and turned to us. "Her father does not like her to go out."

"You mean you can't go to a nightclub but you can go to some stranger's hotel room?" Natasha blurted out to the girl, as if she would be able to understand her.

"Yes," the girl said firmly. She smiled, waved good-bye to us, and moved on to another restaurant with her basket of roses and kid sister.

"By the way," Natasha said to me. "You didn't miss out on anything the other night. Athens beaches aren't that great in my opinion. Too many rocks."

A roofless room. A gigantic bed under the stars. That evening we exchanged our pension room for one on the top floor. It was a ghetto room. Ashtrays and wine bottles were strewn about—souvenirs from the previous guests. There was no railing on the balcony, which fell off to six stories, and the roof only partially covered us. It was like a New York loft, without a top. I had never seen anything like it.

Natasha and I would have to share the bed.

If only my mother had seen this place. I could hear her voice: *What if you walked in your sleep?* In spite of all this, our bed faced the Acropolis and presented the most amazing view of the city I had yet seen, much different than the city view we'd seen with the boys, whose names had by now escaped me. We felt like royalty—popping red grapes into our mouths while gazing at the full south side of the Acropolis, the Parthenon, and the tip of the Porch of the Maidens, the columns sculpted into shapely women with long hair, Natasha's favorite. It was as though I'd just slid on a pair of much-needed glasses.

The beauty of the monuments hadn't yet touched me as they did on this night. The Parthenon stood on a small mountain at the center of the city, now looming above everything else. It was more decayed than the rest of the city, its Doric columns and stones now the color of cinnamon toast. But in the ancient building I saw something else, the only honorable remains of a place now littered with garbage. Perhaps it was a reminder to the citizens of who they were, where they came from, an imposing relic of the first intellectuals to claim art and poetry as noble pursuits. Perhaps it reminded Athenians to open their minds to the questions man had previously feared to ask: what is the nature of art? Of love? Of beauty?

"It looks like a big wedding cake!" Natasha squealed.

The bold structure with its great pillars seemed at once powerful and yet, as Natasha noted, also a wedding cake: creamy colored and detailed. An ancient ruin, as impressive as the Egyptian Pyramids or Stonehenge, while seemingly sad and lost, buried among the modern city of skyscrapers and dirty streets packed tight with apartments, metros, and shops. The Parthenon might have been the city's last hope. How strange, amid these bustling centuries, that an island so peaceful and old-world could still exist.

"It's so passionate," Natasha said, referring to the structure.

Strange science fiction–like sounds came from taxicabs below, layers of Greek music clashing chaotically into noise.

"I don't know much about passion," I said, looking down to the streets.

"You will," Natasha said confidently.

How did she know? I wanted to believe her.

"I have a feeling that it is something involving a mixture of great pleasure and inconvenience." I sighed. And she laughed.

While opening a bottle of wine, I cut my finger on the serrated edge of the bottle opener and my blood began to drip onto the sheets. I didn't have anything to stop the bleeding. Natasha returned from her shower and entered the room, wrapped in a crisp white towel. "Suck it," she advised, catching sight of the blood.

After seeing me cringe at this, she dropped the towel and handed it to me. "Here. Use this. I don't know how you can stand wearing all those clothes, anyway," she said, her body full and confident. She began rubbing lotion into her body, massaging it into every corner and crevice.

I tried not to look.

"You're right. I guess heat rises, even outside."

My finger wrapped tightly in the cloth, the bleeding quickly stopped. I pulled off my pajama bottoms and just wore my underwear. Natasha was right about the clothing factor: it was much more comfortable without them. We stayed up late, drinking chilled Retsina straight from the bottle, our only option in a single star pension that supplied no plastic guest cups.

Retzina wine has a peculiar taste, a bit like turpentine, but it helped keep us cool, and helped cut the taste of garlic we had been accumulating from all the spicy meals. Between sips, Natasha would remind me to lick my finger, to make

sure it was healing. She said it was good to lick my finger
after drinking wine, that the alcohol would cleanse it, despite
the slight sting. Every time she said "lick," I felt my eyes inad-
vertently falling across her flesh, to her peach-colored bra,
silky thin, and matching panties. Perhaps she had bought
them to wear for the knight in shining armor whom she
planned to meet.

I found a pleasure I had never known just in imagining
her body against the moist-looking silk material, a material
that had been made from worms.

As the sun set, lights surrounding the Acropolis glistened
and lit the monuments with spectacular drama. Mosquitoes
nibbled at our skin almost constantly. Finally we'd stopped
slapping them away and just decided to let them go for it:
even the mosquitoes wanted a taste of this heaven.

Natasha brought out a rose-tinted photo of her lover back
in America. His name was Timothy, and he had recently left
her. It was the kind of photo he might have gotten taken on
a whim in a shopping mall, as a gift for his mother. The photo
revealed a slight man with unkempt blond hair, long and
stringy, and a set of devilish eyes. He looked like a surfer or
perhaps an unemployable actor. Someone lazy—too lazy to
love well.

I told her he was handsome.

Sitting on the end of the large bed, combing her wet hair,
the smell of baby lotion permeating the air, Natasha went on
to explain the details of losing her relationship to Timothy,
and how she had lost her virginity to him.

"It was at the Shakespeare festival in Ashland, Oregon.
Ever been?"

I shook my head. She continued to describe the events in poetic detail.

"... in the rear of a rusted gypsy wagon, nestled in straw ..."

"That sounds painful."

"Oh, it was! I bled all over. It was a holy experience ... it was destiny."

"But aren't you destined to meet your soul mate here? Abroad?"

She looked toward the Parthenon and shrugged, setting down her comb to light a cigarette. The light reaching up from the street lamps was just enough to shadow half her face. She smoked her cigarette as though she were sharing a secret with it, blowing out the smoke with a quick exhale and push from her cheeks. She looked like a painting, an image made up of thousands of fervent strokes, which at once became all the photos I had taken of Natasha at her command, photos that I considered too posed. She was a painting of her own design, a posturing self-portrait of everything she wanted everyone to see. But I wanted to capture her simplicity and innocence, assets of hers I wasn't sure she was even aware of.

"I never said Timothy was my soul mate," Natasha continued. "He was more like a messenger dog, a hummingbird sipping from my flower."

I quietly loaded my camera as she lit her cigarette. She was sucking and rolling her cigarette around in her fingers.

"I can't wait to get to Italy," she said. "Maybe my soul mate will be waiting for me there."

Spurred by a sudden confidence in my vision, I decided that in order to be a true artist, I would have to start taking charge of what I saw. I hooked in the flash and snapped her picture. The whole city seemed to explode in light for one moment.

She gasped. "Ah. Why did you do that?"

I forced a smile and effortlessly raised one of my eyebrows, trying my best to feign an apology. "The light was so right, I just had to."

Chapter 4

Goose Bumps

Chariots of whitecaps. Crisp smell of saltwater and warm rushes of sunlight washing our cool cheeks.

Her arm outstretched, her cherubic face detached, Natasha offered to share her apple with me. I took a bite, sensing a possibility, and threw the core to the wind.

Across the Balkan Sea, we took an overnight ferry to San Salvo, Italy, then headed north by train. To the right of our view, palm trees and ocean; to the left, vast vineyards where scattered cottages resided, overlooking their harvest; and beyond this—mountains capped with snow.

We arrived in Venice at dusk. As we got off the train with our bags, I took a deep breath and gazed at a landscape of pastel that matched nothing I'd ever seen in photo books or even in paintings. A great fusion took place between Venice's light and its structures. Lanterns on corners enhanced the rosy warmth of the city's evening color. Terra-cotta walls and roughly hewn wooden windows and door frames were lit by the moonlight, their distorted reflections cast against the slowly stirring canals.

We had to lug all our bags and suitcases ourselves, as there were no taxis at hand. The Grand Canal cut through the city, providing a source for smaller canals. We made our way on foot, since no water buses were available at this time, and automobiles were not an option. Gondolas, as well, were well out of Natasha's budget. We made frequent stops, long enough to peel off an extra layer of clothing courtesy of the sticky Mediterranean air, stuffing the discarded pieces into our bags. We scratched at our mosquito bites, digging our nails into the backs of our knees, along our ankles, and down the lengths of our arms and even our hands. Our dreamy roof-room had exacted a steep price that we were now paying.

We shared an on-the-go meal of boiled nuts, and fed them to each other as we passed the bag. Whoever held the nuts had to feed the other while they carried the map and navigated. While feeding her a cashew, I'd felt Natasha's tongue lick the edge of my finger, and this had sent a chill throughout my body, awakening my skin.

I walked with my head tilted back, observing the way colors aligned on a clothesline beneath the setting sun. Even the placement of a wooden oar on a gondola became a statement of natural beauty. I paused to photograph the image, but Natasha hurried me, growing impatient.

"Come on. I'm tired and hungry. I want to settle in."

I let Natasha choose where we'd stay, since she was the one on the limited budget. She'd apparently been saving tips from waitressing for seven months for this trip, in addition to her birthday money and income tax return, and every dollar, or rather, each "lire," was expended after careful decision. I walked behind her, my luggage significantly heavier than hers, lugging my photography equipment. Sometimes I would look down and notice Natasha's rear leading the way, her full hips and slender waist like a Victorian sylph's. Her legs, stretching out long beneath the serrated hem of her skirt, revealed thick muscular calves, no doubt from waiting tables. Although far from my original intentions, I was beginning to appreciate the detours Natasha's company was affording for this trip— this landscape of body in which my eyes traveled. I had never so courageously looked at another woman.

It was almost intimidating, Natasha's desire to see everything, getting snapshots in front of all the famous landmarks of Venice: the Rialto Bridge, the bell tower, and the great San Moise church of St. Mark's square, the great living room of the city where tourists, pigeons, artists, drinkers, and musicians all gathered. In the square we stopped to read a plaque, conveniently written in English. We learned that the square was not the result of a prearranged plan, but the product of many interventions, beginning during the ninth century.

"Sounds like my chaotic life," Natasha said, her voice edgy, her words clipped. She turned her back to the plaque.

I saw a kind of beauty in this parallel, this courage it took Natasha to live a life fueled by such a loose and natural passion. I also wondered if this was something she regretted, in the same way I regretted my unoriginal life.

As I set up shots, I did my best to avoid the tourists and the telephone wires, which had a way of dating pictures. I was particularly drawn to the phalanx of docked boats, the rows of gondolas whose tips arose from the grim lagoons like oily bat wings—extending out over the concrete edges of the docks, their need to escape hindered by ropes tethered to candy-striped dock poles. Oh, I wanted this summer to be different. I seemed to be waiting for something to happen. Natasha seemed to be waiting, too.

I didn't mind sharing my film anymore. In fact, I was feeling a lightness I hadn't experienced for some time, as when I was a child and would ride my banana-seat bicycle through the country club subdivision, the summer air whipping through my hair as I gazed at all the big houses on the golf course, wondering who lived in them, and waiting for a lonely girl to come running out of one of them to play with me. It never happened, but the prospect had filled me with euphoria. I would have shared my entire summer—the sweet smells of soil that changed with every hour, every shift of wind if only someone had been there with me.

It was not unlike this now, this hyper-awareness of the sky, the weather, and my surroundings, and now the pleasure I was finding in Natasha's company—not just a fantasy. With each day Natasha grew more respectful of my style, of the time I needed to devote to the landscapes I was shooting. Our companionship fell into a natural rhythm that seemed to benefit us both.

One afternoon in Campo S. Rocco, Natasha pulled me into a little costume shop called Gondola that clothed Carnival participants. The interior of the shop was much more lavish than its unassuming facade suggested. Packed with handmade masks, many painted in glitter, some with the red lips and darkened eyes reminiscent of harlequins. Plumed hats ornamented with colored feathers. Hair wreaths of silk eucalyptus decorated with red grapes. Silk gloves. Shapes that were ruffled, conical, and fringed. Colors that combined gold, silver, burgundy, and midnight blue. All vivid. All spectacular. Along the back wall were two large glass cases filled with what appeared to be vintage costumes, even more decadent and extravagant than the new.

Natasha's eyes searched the walls until they fastened upon a mask that had purple tears streaming down one cheek. She took it down and held it to her face, looking at me. "Would you like to join me in the Dance of Death?" she asked in a deep voice.

In response I chose a mask that resembled a bird's head—white, with a long pointed beak and peacock feathers extending from the sides—and held it to my face. "I'm already dead," I whispered, exaggerating my voice as well, something I found surprisingly easy to do behind the mask.

How wonderful was the thought of hiding my identity for a night and parading as someone else. To become whatever I wished. A simple change of clothes could reinvent my body.

Although very different, most of the masks seemed to suggest placidity, their expressions not necessarily lacking in emotion, but appearing somehow lost, or in transition.

What better face for a night of endless possibilities?

"I'd like to wear this when we meet," Natasha said, perhaps referring once again to her famous knight. She held out a crushed red velvet gown from a rack. It had a corset-styled top and a balloon skirt.

From the back curtain emerged the clerk, a tall, dark-haired woman, as sleek as polished silver. She tipped her glasses off her nose, allowing them to drop on their cord to her chest, and walked over to us with a regal air that could only be carried by a woman in her middle years.

"The festival arrives sooner than you think and we get very low on supplies by autumn," she said in clear English. "I'm La Donna and I can explain, if you like, some of the merchandise here that is costlier than you anticipated."

She stood with one hip thrust forward, her hands behind her back, her eyes studying both of us. I noticed she was in excellent shape for her years, with strong shoulders and a slender waist. She seemed the kind of woman who might have married into money and, rather than put her energies into family, had instead focused on fulfilling her personal dreams.

Natasha looked at a price tag on a gown and gasped.

"It took a great deal of work to create the colors for the fabrics in the case." La Donna smiled. "You must understand that Venetian wear is known for its quality. In fact, the quality of the fabric indicates the wealth and social status of its wearer. For example, the purple dye was extracted by crushing thousands of tiny sea snails, and the crimson dye was obtained by crushing a certain type of beetle."

Natasha groaned and wrinkled her nose, disapprovingly.

"People enjoyed what was lavish, in those days, unlike the practicality of our modern times. The more exotic, then, the better." La Donna pointed to a bulletin board on the wall made of velvet and covered with dozens of photographs. "These are some costumes we have sold from past Carnivals," she said.

Natasha walked over and looked at the snapshots closely, squinting her eyes. When I got a good look at the photos myself, I couldn't tell if there were men or women in them, since the costumes created a look of sexual ambiguity.

There was a unicorn mask made of papier mâchè, with cracked alabaster skin, silver leaf, and rhinestones, and a black cone coming from its third eye. A gold overlay covered the eyes and spilled down the long nose, producing a look that was mystical and otherworldly. There was a lion mask made of ceramic, with gold and silver leaf, and velvet cat masks, patterned with stripes and rhinestones.

As we browsed through these artifacts, La Donna explained more about the festival, that it falls just before Lent and that it is the last all-out binge before good Catholics give up all indulgences. She explained that the term "Carnival" was derived from the Latin word meaning "farewell to meat," and that the celebration was modeled on Roman fertility festivals. She described it as a ten-day orgy of pageants, parades, masquerade balls, fireworks, concerts, and *commedia dell' arte*, and told of one woman who adopted a mask for Carnival and hadn't taken it off since.

"If I could be only one face, I would choose the harlequin," Natasha said, pointing to another mask, this time with gold tears streaming down its face. Natasha wore a strange smile. "I've always found a sadness to the masks, and I find myself relating to their sadness."

"Sadness wears well in this city," La Donna intervened, overhearing Natasha's words.

"The women at Carnival look like goddesses," Natasha said and wandered over to a rack of gowns.

It seemed anyone could be beautiful at Carnival. Even the shadow selves were inviting—dressed in black as they were, becoming an unveiling. Strange headdresses made of curtains draped on metal wires loomed along the streets in the pictures on the bulletin board, creating vistas of supernatural possibilities. Some of the photos reminded me a bit of Disneyland with their fairy-tale perfections. Touches of all cultures were mixed here, from Spain to China to India. The costumes said it all, no speech seemed necessary. This was a city made for concealed identity, where one could carry out the secrets of the mind.

"This is the dress of my Carnival fantasy," Natasha suddenly said, then disappeared with it behind the dressing room curtain.

She had succeeded in piquing my curiosity. I longed to know what lurked behind her desires. I stood by the dressing room, waiting. Seeing things through Natasha's eyes had begun to mean more to me than the trip itself.

After a loud rustling, the curtain opened and she emerged—transformed. On her body, the dress had become something different. Along its sides where strings crisscrossed to join the heavy velvet material together, her flesh was now provocatively exposed from beneath her arms all the way to the curve of her hips. She was slender at the waist, and her skin was as pale as the moon. Like powdered mounds of bread dough, her breasts billowed out from the top of the corset. Its gold tassels, lace trim, and fringed skirt put this gown among the most extravagant I'd yet seen. It also came with petticoats beneath the skirt, which Natasha revealed as she walked back and forth, preening and spinning in front of the mirrors.

La Donna nodded approvingly and made a clicking sound much like the men in Greece had made, only this time, Natasha didn't protest. "Venice's artists are known for their distinct blending of the old and new styles," La Donna pointed out, before stepping away to leave us alone with each other.

"Do you know what a challenge it would be to make love in this gown?" she asked, glowing.

She had me help her fasten the back. Her skin was so soft I wanted to run my hands longingly across her.

Perhaps looking like a Gothic princess gave her the confidence to speak more freely than usual with me. "If you found a way inside my skirt you could work your magic without anyone even knowing." She giggled.

I blushed in response to her words which although spoken to me, were no doubt not intended to be taken literally. Nevertheless, I felt a heat rising up inside me, which I hoped Natasha wouldn't notice. I was relieved that she continued to be so absorbed in her reflection that there was no need for me to be apprehensive. I began to lose myself, for the first time in years, in a fantasy. But it was not entirely my own fantasy, being also a fantasy of Natasha's, or rather, what I imagined might be her fantasy.

Natasha, gloriously costumed, would be strolling through the parade, perhaps sipping something strong or licking something sweet, observing the fun and madness, when from the crowd, a hand is placed in her hand. Unaware of where she is being taken, Natasha is led by a cloaked stranger through narrow twisting streets, losing her bearings entirely until they finally arrive at a black door. The stranger draws a key and unlocks the door. Inside the flat all is candlelit, the walls are sanguine in hue. A burst of music blasts in from the street, then all is silent as the door is closed.

The masked stranger looks Natasha up and down slowly, taking time to drink in her beauty. Moving to her, he presses his hands into each nook and curve of her dress, then lightly runs his fingers through her hair. Natasha giggles and starts to remove the mask, but the stranger shakes his head "no" and leads her over to the bed—a wrought-iron, art nouveau–style bed made up with silk sheets and laden with glossy pillows.

Only now does the stranger remove the mask and toss it behind to the hardwood floor. Natasha eyes the man, reaching out to him, dying to know who is about to thrill her beneath her dress. But the mysterious stranger is more mysterious than ever—she is a woman, and turns her face before Natasha can see her, grabbing Natasha's hands and pinning them down to her sides.

The stranger gently presses Natasha back so that she falls back onto the bed. The stranger kneels and begins to lick up Natasha's legs beneath the dress, like a groom in search of a bride's garter belt. Natasha's skin is as soft and pale as one could ever hope—softness that reaches to her panties, tight lacy ruffles that hug her pelvic region. These are tugged down almost instantly by the stranger, who then begins to nibble dutifully at Natasha's thighs, which taste of roses and myrrh.

Finally the stranger begins to ravenously take Natasha's sex into her mouth and lick with a hunger that causes them both to moan. The body of the stranger has become longer, ready to give more, while Natasha has become wet and loose, her legs spread widely. But just as in a fairy tale read to Natasha as a child, the clock tower of the city strikes midnight. Before Natasha has a chance to meet the eyes of her mysterious lover, she slips from between her legs, rises and leaves, exposing as she walks out onto the walkway a long tail of golden hair, curled at its tip. Beneath Natasha's pointed shoes lies the abandoned mask, the bittersweet souvenir she will cherish and savor in the hope of reuniting with its wearer.

Natasha was still gazing at her reflection in the three-way mirror, turning right, left, and then right again.

"I see now that this is not the dress for my Carnival, after all. I would prefer to wear something less restrictive, something I could peel off with one pull. My fantasy is a succulent orgy of multiple lovers, slaves, feeding on my desires. I want no part of me left untouched at my Carnival. I intend to roam the streets, unconcerned about what others think of me for once."

"You may have to have that dress made to order," La Donna said to Natasha, approaching the mirrored area. "And why won't you try a costume?" La Donna asked me. "Are you shy about your body?"

"No," I blurted, and blushed.

"You have a great figure," she said, coming toward me. "Let me see your breasts."

"What was that?" I asked, flushing.

"Your breasts. Let me see them. Then I'll know how to dress them."

Nervously, I unbuttoned my blouse, pushing myself into the unknown, wanting, perhaps, to be more like Natasha.

Natasha stood close by, lips parted, her eyes locked on me.

Finally I unhooked my bra and peered at my freed breasts in the mirror along with the woman. She took one hand and cupped her cool fingers around the base of one of my breasts. I was shocked by her touch and could hardly make out the words that followed.

"You have Jackie Kennedy boobs." She smiled.

"I don't want to show my body," I said. "I want to look, well . . ." I searched for the right words. "Like someone else."

La Donna's voice deepened, becoming almost baritone. "You should wear what you want to wear."

Outside the shop, Natasha and I took deep breaths, relishing the evening air and digesting the past hour in Gondola. I ended up purchasing a black velvet cloak, much like the cloak in my fantasy, and one of the bird masks. The bill was expensive, the purchases unnecessary, but La Donna had been intent upon a sale, and knowing that Natasha couldn't afford a costume, I couldn't seem to escape the fate.

There was a new quiet between us, perhaps because I had surprised her, but I had surprised myself, too.

I spotted a cameo lying faceup on the pavement, similar to the ones from Natasha's watch. I picked it up and handed it to Natasha, a pink helmet shell, so light, it must have been made of plastic.

"Oh, thank you so much!" she said, holding it up to the

empty spot on her watchband, a watch that was obviously dear to her. It touched me that such a worthless item could hold such value to Natasha. "I would have died without it," she exclaimed. "I hadn't even noticed it was gone. Now I'll be able to glue it back."

Natasha noticed so many things, things I wouldn't have thought twice about, much less commented on. We met an elderly postcard salesman on the streets, and she told him what a lovely beard he had; she could barely contain her delight with the seasonings the cook had chosen for the summer squash we'd ordered at a restaurant, and she'd asked our waiter to call the cook out from the kitchen!

I saw how important she made others feel, myself included. I was beginning to realize that she might be privy to a great truth about other people—the meaning they have in our lives, and theirs in ours. She was really living in the world, connecting with others, strangers even.

Thus far, restaurant owners had welcomed us everywhere we went, pulling out chairs for us. Hotel clerks made sure we had rooms that faced the best views, even though these places were only modest pensions. Natasha seemed to bring the best out in all that was around her. Her charm seemed contagious. I began to feel I looked good, too. I felt healthier. My features seemed to soften in mirrors, as well as in the reflection of the canals as we strolled from one tiny island to the next, over the bridges that linked the ancient web of Venice. My tousled blond hair fell around my face in strands, much the way I'd remembered Annie Leibovitz's hair looking when she was working intensely on shoots, intentionally careless of her appearance. I allowed my shoulders to rest and felt genuinely relaxed. It was strange to think that letting go of expectations might actually improve my looks.

One evening, Natasha insisted on combing my hair for me, getting all of the knots out. She started from the bottom and gradually worked the comb through again and again until it came through unfettered. Then she would start over, moving higher until she'd finally reached my scalp. She did this with such gentleness, I found myself becoming excited. I rationalized that this was probably just the way she treated herself, her own hair.

When Natasha had finished, she took me by the shoulders, turning me to face her.

"You're beautiful."

A thought swept through my mind, and terrified me: I almost believed her.

Angelic singing lured us into St. Maria Formosa's cathedral to discover a choir giving a midday concert. At the rear of the church, Natasha and I sat on the marble floor. She gripped my hand as we listened.

There were about a dozen singers: a mature soprano, a male tenor with a gorgeous vibrato, and other individual voices making their way to my ears.

Her hand was warm and smaller than mine, yet more powerful. I tried to make sure I didn't grip it too firmly, but I didn't want to seem lifeless, either. Somewhere, a balance existed between being sure of myself and not giving myself away.

I watched Natasha as she listened, her neck moving along with her breathing. Something like spirit filled the room; the candle flames illuminated the stained-glass windows. The song intensified. Tiny prayer candles filled either side of the narthex, and clustered before the shrines and statuettes, flickering shadows against the church walls. Frankincense and myrhh smoked from heavy bronze containers. *This is how churches should always be experienced,* I thought. *By candlelight at night, holding hands with mystery.*

I knew this concert was something Natasha would be proud to add to her European Experience, but I also could detect a sense of boredom in her posture as she took a deep breath and expanded her chest, sitting up straight as if forcing her attention to the performance, trying to keep herself awake. Her shoulders would soon fall again, and her eyes would drift back over to the door, then down to her watch. Not that I was any more attentive—watching her not watching the performance. In my desire to keep her amused, I finally suggested that we leave.

"I could have stayed longer, but I don't want to burden you with my whims," she said, as we walked back toward our pension, still hand in hand. The intimacy of our bodies touching felt awkward to me, made me self-conscious. But yet here I was, refusing to let go of her hand. I wondered whose intention it had been to keep holding on, and hoped it was both of ours.

I squeezed her hand, feeling her soft skin radiate with heat, wishing I had the nerve to kiss it.

On our last day in Venice, Natasha and I woke to the sounds of singing, like a serenade, an elderly woman hanging out her laundry, singing at the top of her lungs. She had a terrible voice but it was so utterly expressive that it lifted my mood.

We toured the glass factory in Murano, then tried tiramisu ice cream, which tasted like mocha-flavored whipped cream, fluffy and nearly nonexistent, yet something we couldn't have lived without. We tried to memorize the names of the squares that we kept running into again and again on our walks: Dorsoduro, San Polo, Castello. And all the smaller Campos: Campo S. Angelo, Campo Francesco, Campo San Lorenzo.

It was difficult for me to shoot around the tourists in their gaudy T-shirts and fluorescent visors, but I managed to capture some good shots of the building facades, especially a series of shots from a gondola ride, which I insisted on paying for.

It was on this particular gondola ride that Natasha began to seriously pose for me and I discovered how photogenic she was. Her deep-set almond eyes, elegant nose and generous mouth produced an excellent profile as she sat in the foreground of the shots. Although she assumed I would want to snap portraits of her looking at me, smiling, I preferred her staring away from the lens, candid, exposed, and private. It was these shots, taken off guard, that kept making her turn to me saying, "But I wasn't smiling." I knew those would be the photos I would keep.

And then she surprised me.

"This gondola is fit for decadence. Look at it. Red carpet. Gold oars." Her eyebrows were raised as high as I had ever seen them, as if waiting for a response. She crossed her hands around her waist and pulled off her top, revealing her ivory voluptuousness in broad daylight.

I nearly dropped my camera in the water.

In interviews I had read, famous photographers would often comment that at times it is best to just shoot and mull over the meaning and consequences later, but I couldn't bring the camera to my face. I couldn't look at Natasha. Instead, I noticed the gondolier look back and begin sighing, nearly dropping his oar as a series of "Ooh la-la's," sprang forth.

I stood up, my knees shaking as the narrow boat began to rock a little. Standing in front of Natasha so that the man couldn't see her, I accidentally brushed my hand against her breasts as I did so, and I quickly apologized. She pushed me to the side and made a sour face, aimed at the rower. She gave him the finger.

As though this happened to him every day, the rower shrugged and turned back to the canal and started singing an Italian melody that reminded me of "La Vie en Rose." Natasha remained in her seated position, her half-naked body stretched out. A slight breeze swept our way as the gondola turned its course, heading back the way we had traveled.

"Hurry." Natasha smiled, goose bumps standing on her arms. She looked ready to be captured.

Luckily, we were moving into a quiet section of the city, a small canal lined with houses, a church, and few opening vistas where tourists would pass.

The sky was slightly overcast, causing the sunlight to appear soft and hazy, as though we were in a dream. Natasha kicked off her sandals and lay back on the red-carpeted sofa, her breasts falling back onto her and spreading out, her barefoot toes up on the gunwales of the boat.

"That dress we saw in the Carnival shop," she said. "I'm going to wear something like that when I meet him. That's how it's going to be."

She looked away from me, from the camera, stretched her neck out, face to the afternoon sun, and closed her eyes. She looked more peaceful than I'd ever seen anyone look in my entire life. The weight of my camera became nonexistent, a kind of third eye. I was able, for the first time, to really look at Natasha without fear of being "found out." I realized that it was *I* who was seeing inside of *her*, and that I was seeing something nobody else could see, not even Natasha.

She couldn't afford that dress. Even I couldn't afford that dress.

I captured her slightly overexposed, a contrast against the passing backdrops: lavender- and mauve-painted town houses, fresh flowers cascading from balconies, sun-bleached laundry swaying on the lines strung across the narrow alleyways. The gondola slipped past golden doors, swaying along gated walls, the shiny *fero* (the metal bar decorations at each boat's tail) rising high into an afternoon sky. I wanted shots powerful enough to hold Natasha's beauty, yet I knew that in order to get them, I had to remain distant since if my thoughts became erotic, which they easily could have, they would risk infecting the portraits.

If I'd known this was going to happen, I would have bought grainier film, I thought; something more modest, less harsh and revealing. But I was aware that I was not in control of the moment, it was controlling me. I was merely the medium, dutifully participating in the inevitability of the scene. I was documenting. I tried to stand as far away from her as I could within the confines of the boat. I was using my wide-angle lens so as to not exploit her curves. I wanted to portray her as a painting, fragmented, in a sense.

I didn't know how I would develop these prints in the school lab. Fears rushed through my mind that someone would look into one of the developing buckets and see what I had been up to. And what would I do with the photos, once printed? Certainly I wouldn't share them.

The boat swayed.

"Don't fall in." She laughed.

Each time the camera clicked, something inside me seemed to be saying "yes." I thought about how dangerous it would feel to be beautiful, to possess a beauty that could purchase such freedom, to allow me to share so much of myself with others. Natasha opened her eyes and looked at me with an obvious seriousness, as though she had just read my thoughts. I imagined that this was how lovers felt, that they spoke some silent language.

Tears gathered below Natasha's lashes, and she set down the receiver. It was raining and we were in a phone booth now, our hot breath filling the confines with steam. I wrapped my arms around her and felt a surge of energy pass between us. Everything became so quiet I noticed the silence as though it were a sound, and all I could hear was the rush of raindrops against the glass.

Natasha began to cry harder. Her cat had died. "I knew this would happen to him if I went away." She wept, wiping away her tears, her bracelets jingling on her wrist.

She looked lovely when she cried, shaking her head so that her hair fell into her face. I was ashamed to be so aware of her physicality while she was in pain, dispassionate to her situation as I was. Yet she had a face that seemed to erase the idea that true pain could even exist, carrying a wild beauty along with her sorrow. Secretly, naively of course, like the viewers of great gothic films and soap operas, I longed for that same kind of pain.

It rained until the world outside the windows blurred. I thought for a moment how wonderful it would be to stay there with Natasha, inside that glass box, our world slowed and softened by the pampering sounds of nature, as though we were nestled inside a womb. I recalled during the previous winter in Los Angeles when it had rained. I was driving home from the supermarket, the sounds of rain against my car massaging my ears, the windshield wipers creaking back and forth for the first time in months. Dark patches of sky loomed over Beverly Hills, the horizon closing in. I pulled into the driveway and turned the engine off, deciding not to get out of the car right away, and closed my eyes. My body felt warm and protected inside the car—lulled into relaxation by the thrumming of rain against the roof. I fell asleep. I woke later to the sound of my mother rapping on the passenger side window. She was confused as to why I was sleeping in the car and not in my own bedroom, and upset that I hadn't brought the groceries in, complaining that she couldn't understand how I could have fallen asleep. I couldn't tell her then that letting go and allowing my body to sleep where I wanted at that moment was a freedom I craved and deserved, that I'd wanted to stay in that car all night, listening to the storm.

Covering our heads, Natasha and I ran from the booth, the cool rain soaking our bodies within seconds, and darted into a café on the corner that was full of striking young Italian men drinking bottled beer. Within moments we found ourselves letting them hold us up in the air, in celebration of a soccer game they were watching on a battered television set suspended from the ceiling. This seemed to cheer Natasha a little.

Outside, the rain had stopped, but the sky was still dark and gray, and we were quickly losing light. Overwhelmed by the labyrinth of cobblestone bridges that linked together the one hundred and eighteen tiny islands of Venice, we lost our way back to the hotel. We knew going without a map in

Venice was a daunting proposition—potentially fatal in terms of reaching one's destination. A kind stranger surprised us each with a rose as he passed, so Natasha and I stopped at one of the bridges where she proposed we make wishes and toss our flowers into the water. She said that wishes worked best when sung.

"I believe in wishing," she said. "And wishes like a melody."

"You go ahead. I'm afraid I'll have to sit this one out."

"You sit everything out," she said. "I won't allow it any-more."

"I won't sing, Natasha."

"Then choose the song and I'll sing it."

"I don't know any new music. I listen to oldies: Billie Holiday, Cole Port—"

"Name a song."

"Oh, I don't think you will know any of them."

"What is your favorite song?"

I paused. "You sing your song first."

It took her a while to think of a song. She closed her eyes while she searched for the words, then slowly the song came. *"Et quand dans la nuit tout s'endormit. Je vis les cieux devant mes yeux fermes, Dans le silence . . ."*

Her voice was light and high, almost operatic, just as I imagined it to be, only with a gentleness that I hadn't imagined until now. Perhaps she was singing a lullaby? Although her French was lovely, I couldn't understand most of the words, but they were soothing nonetheless. How appropriate that she would choose a song that I couldn't quite under-stand.

She gazed down into the lagoon, her expression turned sad and contemplative. *"Meme s'il fait noir . . ."* The song had to do with embracing darkness. I pretended that it was meant for me.

Finally, her head tilted to one side, she finished the song. *"Dans la nuit,"* she said, releasing her rose into the canal. "It means, 'In the night.'"

Unable to bring myself to sing, I simply made a wish and tossed the rose into the canal, hoping my efforts would prove sufficient to Natasha's request.

The landscape had grown dark and everything was beginning to look the same. The canals were flooding from the evening rain. I couldn't remember the names of the squares anymore. My shoes were wet, as some of the squares we had walked through had become flooded.

"This place is sinking into the sea," Natasha said, stopping to roll up her pants. "Slowly rotting away."

Somehow, during our walk back, we ended up making one great circle, to find ourselves back at our pension. I was disappointed—tonight it seemed I could walk for miles. I didn't want the evening to end. But Natasha marveled at our arrival at the pension. "Look what a great sense of direction we have!" She was obviously ready to call it a night. "I'm dead to ring the walls."

I looked out into a shimmering canal that trailed into soft darkness. Gondolas rocked sleepily at its edges, looking like a shadowy postcard. I thought about what a perfect moment I was standing in, a moment surrounded by great beauty and poetry, with a woman who said things like "dead to ring the walls," instead of a simple word like "tired."

"This would be the perfect place to die," I finally said.

Natasha came over to me and touched my back with her

fingertips. I could feel her long nails through the cotton shirt I was wearing.

"There must be something else you want," she whispered.

I thought about this for a while. "I want to end up somewhere else."

"Where?" she probed, lightly running her nails across my shoulders, then down my back. My clothes had become transparent to her touch, my skin was alive. "We've mapped out this city. We can find our way anywhere if we try. Where would you like to go?"

I had read about lovers getting lost in Venice, and I suppose the idea had always appealed to me. I envisioned it like something out of a film, as though it would lead me on an adventure and in the end, change my life.

"I want to go somewhere I've never been. I want to get lost."

"Not tonight," she said as she grabbed my hand and guided me back to our room.

Before falling asleep, I lay in bed next to her, filled with what can only be described as a type of ecstasy. Although the bed was wide enough to fit us both comfortably, long strands of her hair feathered across my shoulder, as Natasha's back was to me. Her hair was soft and curled, and tickled my skin in a way that caused the tiny hairs on my arms to stand up. We were both in our panties again, only now she slept without her bra, perhaps because I had seen so much of her already. Perhaps not. Her back was eggshell pale and there were dark beauty marks, like rubies on tulle, just below her shoulder blades, the bones I'd always called Wings. I could smell the warmth of her body, under her arms, sweet and delicious like baby powder or candy-scented deodorant.

"Italy has turned out to be quite a surprise," I whispered.

Her body stirred and she stretched her legs, so that one leg pressed against mine. Her toe slid up my shin and then back down. My entire body shivered.

"Paris will be much better," she said, and drew her leg back from mine.

Chapter 5

Breeding Grounds

But even Paris took a backseat to Natasha's demands. Although it was not on our route, we went to Amsterdam first, taking an entire day out of our way just so Natasha could experience Amsterdam's "coffee shops." I had not protested at the Amsterdam detour, and now I would have to live with the consequences. I decided that my way of surviving the next twenty-four hours would be to view it as if it were a fateful adventure.

After an overnight train ride, we arrived early enough to witness the city's stench and grime by dawn, while the canals were empty and the houses still slept. We were strolling through the streets along the Singel, which was the canal running about the Centrum, the center of Amsterdam.

"I want to be naughty tonight," Natasha said, grinning mischievously and stretching her body.

I, too, felt the need to unwind after our long train ride. Wide open towards sex, self-expression, and soft drugs, the underlying feel of Amsterdam was one of youth. In a space less than a mile in diameter, we were surrounded by bars, clubs, coffee shops, brothels, and a lingering haze of mari-

juana smoke. Nicknamed the Venice of the north, Amsterdam
was made up of small plots of land surrounded on all sides by
canals. But so far, nothing resembled the Venice we had just
left. I tried to coax Natasha away from this seedy neighborhood,
into the Herengracht, the Keizersgracht, and the Prinsengracht,
where the taverns, restaurants, and shops were more diversi-
fied, but Natasha insisted we stay where the tourists were.

"Do you realize how much there is outside of Amsterdam?"
I asked Natasha. "Like tulip fields and windmills," I started, pulling out my guidebook.

"True travelers don't rely on guidebooks," Natasha said,
reaching over and closing the pages I was leafing through.
"Trust your instincts. Let them be your guide. Amsterdam is a
place to party."

My stomach turned over, nervously. It looked as if I had a
long night ahead.

Natasha gave me a disapproving look. "Don't bother trying to coax me into a day of museums. Not in this town. It's
sex, drugs, and rock and roll here. And I plan to live it up."

We spent our entire day in the Red Light District, an area
my guidebook strongly recommended avoiding, pointing out
that it was both seedy and dangerous.

It was sunny and the air was warm and still, without a
breeze. Despite the bluish sky, a fog hung over the canals and
set a tone I chose to view as romantic rather than depressing.

We strolled along, munching on Dutch Toblerone choco-
lates and pointing out to each other the more shocking signs
in the windows, promoting sex and drugs. A part of me was
titillated by the signs, as long as Natasha didn't press us to
enter the buildings. So far, we'd only been window shopping.
But my luck was running out.

We stopped at Café Weiner, despite its empty parlor, because its name amused Natasha. At our table, Natasha asked to see a menu and the waiter soon emerged with two laminated poster cards displaying photos of various types of weed. Natasha ordered two servings and the server quickly returned with a big box containing marijuana, paper, tobacco filler, and a book of matches.

I photographed her rolling joints. As she focused on the intricacy of finishing them, she pursed her lips with an earnestness I had not yet seen in her, lacing each cigarette with hash, then licking the paper clean. I also shot her lighting hers up, inhaling, smiling, and finally exhaling. She appeared to be in her element inside the shop, which was still barren except for the bartender, myself, and the Pink Floyd songs playing from a jukebox—her choice of music.

I ordered French fries and a beer. The fries came topped with a messy dollop of mayonnaise. Natasha's eyes were now half closed, the dramatic black liner along her upper lids making her look like Cleopatra.

"You can't just not experience this," Natasha said, inhaling another long drag off her joint. "I'm your guide, okay? You need to do what I say."

With this she shoved a joint into my fingers and winked at me. My resistance melted. With no plausible excuse for denying her, I sucked the hash in and held it for a few moments, until my lungs felt as if they might explode. Pink Floyd suddenly became not rock but New Age to me, and I wondered why I'd never really listened to it before. Natasha and I both took off our cardigans, enjoying the sensation of the air-conditioning fanning our shoulders from above our heads. I helped Natasha unwrap the scarf from around her neck. As I did so, I noticed the contrast of her hair against the white silk scarf, marveling at how truly red her hair was.

Natasha offered me the joint again, and as good as I was feeling, I decided to pass. She pouted at me.

"Later," I promised.

"Have you smoked pot before?"

"A little," I said. It was another of my white lies this summer. But it seemed like the best route toward gaining her respect: if I could present myself as more experienced, I felt I would be better justified to go at my own pace.

Oak bar. Licorice syrup. Plumes of sweet-smelling smoke reflected in mirrors. The bar had gradually become filled with a mixture, it seemed, of both locals and tourists. Natasha kept the jukebox playing on every Pink Floyd song they had.

We ordered Jagermeister shots with Heineken beer backs, and Natasha nursed hers down with countless puffs of blond hash, followed by cigarettes. The Café Wiener's prices were outrageous, and I was surprised at how quickly Natasha was putting her money down, more quickly than I'd yet witnessed her doing.

Our night in the Red Light District suddenly got slow. Everything had begun to flow with a sticky tempo, like the lingering, sweet, licorice-tinged shots the bartender kept pushing to us.

"You know this has opium in it, don't you?" Natasha said.

The bartender overheard Natasha's comment and claimed that it was no longer true. But Natasha argued with him and finally, he smiled and winked and let her be.

Two Dutch men in trench coats, one resembling an older, worn-out Kiefer Sutherland, passed us their joint and asked us about our evening plans. I passed again on the joint and avoided eye contact with them, hoping they'd just leave us be. I feared us having another night like we'd had at the lookout mountain in Athens, where I would be forced to watch Natasha foolishly try to entertain an audience who cared for only one thing.

"Did anyone ever tell you that you were remarkably uptight?" asked the younger of the two men in a thick Danish accent. His ability to quickly size me up made him obviously not the fool I'd taken him for.

I shivered in embarrassment, turning my face away from the men and looking towards the door. As I watched a few women leave the bar, I thought about following them and just returning to the hotel by myself.

"Yes," Natasha slurred. "Danielle is remarkable. But the uptight part is just a façade."

I wasn't sure where Natasha was going with this or who she was now aiming to please more, the men or me.

"It's a façade I intend to burn down," she finished, then tried to light herself another cigarette until the older gentleman intervened, motioning for her to wait.

"And how do you propose to do this?" he asked, raising a brow as he pulled out a red electric lighter and held it out for Natasha.

After a closer look, I found the older man more attractive than I had originally thought. In fact, there was a subtlety to both men that I found rare and rather intriguing.

"I'm not sure yet," Natasha finally answered, blowing out a puff of smoke, her head leaning to one side in contemplation. "I was thinking that maybe we would see a sex show."

Both men chuckled.

"Those aren't erotic," said the younger of the two men.

The older one cleared his throat. "We should let the ladies be the judge of that."

"All right," Natasha said to them.

"How much are they? Will you take us to one?"

The men explained that sex shows were actually quite expensive, but that there was a little theater just around the corner showing X-rated films.

"Fine," Natasha said. She stood, wobbling a little, betraying her intoxicated state, and offered a wry smile. "Take us, boys. What are you waiting for?"

Outside, the weather had changed. A dark sky of rain-swollen clouds loomed, and cold winds were blowing in from all directions. Luckily, the men offered us their trench coats. Natasha and I looked like detectives in them and I had one of the men take our photo near the canal. Mosquitoes flew out from the edges of the water, swarming at our elbows and knees. Avoiding the canals, we stayed near the buildings instead.

As we walked, I made a point of keeping my distance from the men, wanting them not to get their hopes up, and hoping to set an example for Natasha. Drunk, Natasha leaned on the arm of Kiefer for support.

I wished the night were already over and dreaded the hours I knew were to follow, hours I was sure were going to get worse.

We soon arrived at a small building wedged tightly between other stores and located in a narrow, cobblestone alley. We entered the theater and found a place to sit near the back, but Natasha quickly insisted we move up toward the front to assure us a good view of the screen. The film reels started in Dutch, with no subtitles, but the meaning was not lost on us.

As the film progressed, depicting acts that became increasingly unappetizing, Natasha became restless. Finally, she looked over at me, her mouth turned down in a frown. "What are we doing here? This is disgusting."

I was bewildered that she was asking me this question, I who would never have been there if not for her. But I didn't have time to answer.

She grabbed at my arm and hissed, "I'm not feeling well." Then, stepping over our escorts, she got up and went to the bathroom.

After a few minutes, I followed and found her vomiting in the sink. I brought her a wet wad of paper towels and she cleaned her face, peering at her reflection in the mirror, a lipstick-smeared face and two slits for eyes.

"I need to go pass out," she said.

We'd left the trench coats with the doorman and asked him to give them back to the escorts we had ditched. Apart from Natasha's discomfort, the night was turning out better than I had anticipated. We were almost back at our hotel and ready to call it a night when she stopped dead in the center of the road. "Oh, no, I forgot my scarf back at the bar. My good scarf!"

"But we are almost at our hotel. Do you know how far we've walked?" I protested.

She looked at me, confused, tired, and leaned on me in exasperation. Her face was hot and I blew against it, trying to cool her, and patted her back as though she were a sick child.

She pulled away, raising an eyebrow, and stated firmly, "I won't leave this city without it."

I nodded, assuming we would retrieve it in the morning, until I remembered that our train tickets had already been purchased and we were scheduled to leave tomorrow morning. The thought of missing our train filled me with dread. We would have to stay in Amsterdam another day. I wanted to get this detour over with and never have to look at this filthy place again.

"I'll get your scarf," I volunteered.

"Alone? In this city? What would your mother think?"

"I'll be fine, Natasha. You need to rest."

She stumbled and yawned. "Why are you so sweet to me?" she asked.

I just smiled. "I'll see you back in our room," I said.

I turned to head back to the bar, longing for my comfortable bed where I could pull the covers over my head in my crisp air-conditioned room at home. I wanted to escape this city that claimed to be erotic, but was, in my view, nothing more than a frat-house party, minus the good-looking students. The only thing that kept me going was thinking that I would never be here again.

Walking along, I came upon a row of windowed caverns, lit with colored lights. *Live erotic performances. Bisexuals, threesomes, and banana shows! Vibrators, dildos, and more!* I felt as if I were at a circus, only, thank God, my mom wasn't here to hold my hand. Billboards and neon lights invited passersby like me to participate in Amsterdam's mischief. I must have taken a wrong turn, I thought, because I couldn't recall this depraved strip of storefronts.

There stood a prostitute beneath the lights, with long wavy black hair, a beautiful face, and a nearly flat chest. She appeared to be drunk. She raised her glass to me and winked, shifting her weight to lean forward and ask me, through a hole in the glass, if I would like to come in. She must have known I was from America, because she spoke to me in English.

"No, thank you," I said as I passed. Surprisingly, the offer had not unnerved me.

"Then come again sometime, and ask for Scarlett," she said, with an unexpected southern accent. "I'll be waitin'." I nodded and hurried on.

"We take requests," a man shouted out to me from the entrance of his club. "Tell the hostess what you want to see, and she'll make sure you get your request. You want to see the couple fuck doggy? They'll do doggy. We have three alternating couples."

Again, I passed, rather surprised that I was not offended by the offers. Because they were strangers to me, I felt a freedom that I normally wouldn't have. After all, what they did had nothing to do with me.

I almost wished I would run into the two Dutch men from Café Weiner again so that they could be my guides. Thinking about them now, they didn't seem so bad. In fact, the younger one had been rather charming and had been dressed exceptionally well beneath his coat.

Finally I reached the Café Weiner. I found the bartender who had waited on us and asked him if he'd seen Natasha's scarf. When he said he had, I felt relief, only to tense up again at his next words.

"But it's not here now. We have all our lost-and-found items taken over to a larger club that stays open after we close. The owner was just here and left with them. You have to go to the Roxy to get it."

"Are you kidding? The scarf is gone already?"

"Sorry. Most people never come back for their items anyway. People get so drunk they forget where they leave their things."

"All right," I said. "Can you direct me to the Roxy?"

"Sure, but perhaps you should wait until tomorrow. It's Party Night at the Roxy and it may not be your cup of tea, if you know what I mean."

Party Night translated into Another Day for me. I wanted to leave. I would rather be drinking in Paris. So I got directions from him and made my way through the windy streets.

Several times, I became confused and had to ask strangers for directions.

People knew the Roxy. And most people spoke English. I noticed that several people grinned at me knowingly when I mentioned the name of the club. A part of me was tempted to explain the circumstances, that I wasn't seeking out this notorious club because of any personal interest, but I restrained myself and decided to try their assumptions on for size. It was certainly making my world look different for a night.

I finally made it to the Roxy. The club was large, located in the hulking shell of an old movie theater. As I entered I found myself anticipating whatever was happening inside with heightened interest.

I actually wanted to be shocked.

The door to the entrance was closed. I walked up and gave it a knock. I was the only one standing outside. I even wondered if the club was open.

A window in the door was suddenly opened, revealing the bald head of a man in his thirties. He had large empty holes in his earlobes, like African ear spacers. The man silently waited, observing me.

"May I come in?"

"No," he said bluntly, then slammed the window shut.

Stunned by his abrupt rejection of me, I had no idea what to do next.

"Don't waste your time," I heard an American voice from behind me say, by way of explanation.

I turned to find two men standing nearby, smoking cigarettes and shaking their heads. They looked like fraternity boys, with their preppy clothes, baseball hats, and tans, the kind of guys my mother would like to see me with.

"We couldn't get in either. I don't give a shit, anyhow," one said distainfully. "This place is for fags and dikes."

"Yeah?" I asked.

I wondered why they were so interested in continuing to hang around a place that they disapproved of. On a whim, I decided to ask.

"We're Americans," they answered. "We're here to see the freaks."

The idea that I was like these men, Americans feeding off the sexual proclivities of others for entertainment, disgusted me. I made up my mind to be a true traveler. I knocked again.

The bald man opened the window. Seeing me, he rolled his eyes, annoyed. "Yes?"

"I'm gay," I said loudly.

He gave me the once-over again, this time taking a bit more time. Did he believe me? I wondered if I should try to stand a certain way, or assume a certain expression in order to pass. Was I dressed appropriately to be considered a lesbian?

I batted my eyes at him.

There was a brief pause. "It's not for gays." Once again he closed the door, though slightly less vehemently this time.

I knocked again and seconds later, the window reopened. "What now?"

"Can I please come in?" I begged, ready to explain about the scarf if I had to.

"Tarts only," he said.

"I just need to see the—"

He cut me off. "Suck my dick?"

"Pardon?"

"Suck my dick."

I nearly laughed outright, I was so startled. But I had no intention of being turned away, and I figured I really had nothing to lose but experience. I'd sucked dick for far less than a scarf.

"Okay."

The man smiled. "You're in. Just leave your panties at the second door."

He opened the door and as I moved toward him, he chuckled and pulled down his jeans, revealing a thick cock with a metal rod spearing right through its head. It was such a shock to me, I became immediately sympathetic to him and had the urge to just question him about whether or not the piercing still hurt. But before I had the chance, the bouncer was being called back to the window.

Making my way along the inside corridor, I spotted a basket of what indeed appeared to be underwear. I peeled off my panties and threw them into the pile with the others, and continued down the corridor.

Inside, the club was hopping. It was crowded with people finding chairs, grabbing drinks, making out. Men and women dressed in fetish attire, circled around a floor stage in the center of the main room. The lights were low, a spotlight traveled on the stage.

After I retrieved the scarf I decided to see what was happening on the stage. To my surprise, there didn't seem to be all that much around me that was so risqué. It simply seemed like a party.

I tossed the scarf around my neck and threaded my way to a place where I, too, could see the stage. There were still some people in between me and what was happening there, which made me feel somewhat protected.

I peered around them. Beneath the rosy light was a woman lying back on her elbows, her legs lifted and spread, showing off her vagina for all to see. She was shorn of any pubic hair, her completely bald, smooth lips seemed swollen and engorged. Perhaps she was already fully aroused.

A striking Asian man came onto the stage and lay down

in front of her, eagerly cupping his mouth over the woman's vagina and blowing on it. This made the woman whimper in pleasure. I began to feel wet just watching, remembering that I had no panties on, longing for what that woman was experiencing. I, too, wanted a tongue to travel across my surfaces. My lips. My breasts. I thought about the others in the room and wondered if they were feeling as aroused as I was.

At one point the people sitting in front of me left, leaving me exposed to the stage. The couple had finished their sex act and had begun to make rounds of the audience. The woman came by and swiped the scarf from my neck, wrapping it around her body for a moment before handing it back to me with a lascivious smile.

I left the stage area and ordered a drink, quickly becoming high. They must have been serving doubles. I ordered another and chatted with an Englishman with a missing tooth. He said his name was Turbo, which stuck with me because who names their son Turbo? He removed his shirt, claiming he was hot. The music was crazy, disco-like and loud, and I couldn't understand a word of the lyrics. I didn't care. I peered about the bar area, still fancying the thought of running back into the two men from Café Weiner. This time I fantasized them playing much more than the part of tour guides, and envisioned them approaching me and engulfing me into their trench coats. It was a mysterious thought that held no sexual clarity, but excited me nonetheless. Turbo held his shirt out next to his hip, like a toreador, daring me to charge him. I danced right through it, not quite knowing what I was doing. The room grew hot and I noticed a couple of women peeling their blouses off. I wished I could take off my top, too, and was about to but instead, decided to leave. On my way out, I was once again greeted by the bouncer.

"You still haven't paid your admission," he hollered to me over the music. He held the same stern-faced expression that he had earlier. I now found it funny, and this turned me on.

He pulled me a couple steps away from the doorway so that the overhead light was no longer directly on us. Eagerly now, I fell to my knees and unzipped his corduroy pants. I ran my hand softly along the elastic of his underwear, and then slipped my hand inside to discover a shaved pubic area with a slight stubble of growth. I pulled his already hard cock out and again observed what I had seen earlier; a large silver rod penetrating his thick head.

Again, I felt excitement for the newness of the accessory, this time wondering what it might feel like inside of me. I wasn't ready to find out, but I couldn't resist at least wrapping my lips around him and tasting the contrast of hot flesh and cool metal. Excitedly, I widened my mouth and began to slide my tongue down to his base, just above his balls, and then playfully licked them. He shuddered and moaned and pressed my head back toward his penis, urging me to continue.

I worked back up his length, all lips and tongue, until I reached his smooth head where the silver piece was. I began to softly suck him.

"You little fucking tart," he said loudly and gripped the back of my hair. He pulled my head back so that I was forced to look into his eyes as he spoke. "You're not such a Jane after all, are you?"

He released his grip and I let my mouth fall back over him, my tongue soaking him with wetness, my lips softly gripping his length as I found a vertical rhythm. Quickly his breathing became loud enough to drown out the music. His body shook against me.

Once he began to come, I replaced my mouth with my

hand and directed his warm semen to fall onto the concrete floor below me. With the music from the club still blaring, I stood up, amazed that no one had interrupted our short affair.

We both straightened ourselves and nodded goodbye to each other as though nothing had happened.

I stumbled back along the deserted streets toward our room, stopping at a café called The Cobbled Way, where I ate soup and crackers.

I remember realizing how drunk I was when I mistakenly asked for directions to our Venice Hotel, slurring my words. Finally, I arrived at the Hotel Cabool. Natasha was passed out. The mattress I fell onto was hard and misshapen and the room was spinning. But I felt good as I drifted off, knowing I had made friends with a foreign city.

Natasha snores. It was late, nearly noon, and we had missed the train.

After all I'd gone through.

I drew back the blinds, to reveal three feet of garbage piled in front of our atrium window. Empty wine bottles, beer bottles, food wrappers, even discarded underwear. No wonder the shades were kept pulled shut.

Natasha suddenly woke up. Immediately, she pulled off her clothes. "These clothes smell disgusting," she said, flinging them across the room.

I could smell her body.

"I haven't washed in two days," she said. "And there are no private showers here. I won't set foot in a shared bathtub. That's how you get athlete's foot."

My mother would have approved of Natasha at this moment, I thought.

Natasha moved about our bedroom, gathering together some clean clothes, her hairbrush, and her wallet. She stroked her fingers lightly across her stomach, looking pensively out at the mess of garbage. I couldn't take my eyes off her, especially the patch of dark-auburn pubic hair that lay just below her belly button, twined like hot wires into a small mass. I wondered what it would be like to see her shaved, like the woman from last night. I wondered what her vagina looked like up close.

"There's my scarf," she said, snatching it off my nightstand.

She wrapped it around her body, bringing it up to her nose. I worried that the scent of the woman from last night might have been left on it, but apparently, it wasn't.

Natasha took a deep breath, closed her eyes, then opened them back up, looking at me with a slight grin.

"You still drunk?" she asked.

I nodded. It was true, I was.

"Amsterdam isn't what I thought it would be," she commented.

The rest of our stay fell back into a familiar rhythm. We toured Anne Frank's house, as well as the sex museum, where Natasha found inspiration in an original seventeenth century chastity belt, as well as a six-foot-long plaster penis. Then, before leaving Amsterdam, Natasha bought a pipe for her friend back home.

In the end, she lost her scarf again, at some other café, but we didn't bother to go back for it this time. She never bothered to inquire about the adventure I'd had in retrieving the scarf the night before, so I never told her.

"I've seen enough of the erotic city," she said.

★ ★ ★

Back on the train, my backpack at my feet, my jacket on my lap, I was still slightly hungover from two nights ago. New fears swirled inside me. I felt far away from myself, and far away from home.

Chapter 6

Fresh Cafe

Paris street. Small cars squeezed into alignment. Triangular intersection with phone booth jutting out almost in front of oncoming traffic.

"Don't go out late with that girl you're traveling with. Do fun things during the day. Don't waste your wonderful trip going to bars. You're in Paris. Live it up!"

Mother had no idea what an oxymoron her statement was, nor had she ever been supportive of my female friends. She was much more unforgiving towards them than she'd ever been with the boys I'd seen, always fond of my boyfriends, so long as I had one. My female friends and neighbors she monitored closely, checking in on us frequently, listening in on our private conversations, and commenting on them after they would leave the house, disapproving of their attitudes and "intuiting" their natures as "untrustworthy." I could remember times when I would be playing cards or watching a movie with a girlfriend, enjoying our time together, when Mother would interrupt to insist she needed me to help her with dinner, and that it was time for my friend to go home. After the girl would leave, Mother would gossip about her,

her lack of class, or her stupidity. It was as though Mother was jealous—not of my time apart from her, but of my pleasure. I'd finally stopped having women friends altogether.

As she continued to speak loudly through the telephone receiver, I turned the volume down and allowed my eyes to wander out to Natasha, standing in the square, waiting for me to finish the call. She carried a notebook under one arm, her cigarette dangling from her fingers. Sturdy pillars in front of a library cast dramatic gray shadows across the ground where she stood. A couple was making their way to a nearby restaurant, when they stopped in the center of the road and kissed, the man taking the woman by her head and pulling her face into his, kissing all over her cheeks and mouth and eyes. The girl was laughing. I watched Natasha smile, drop her cigarette, and take out her notepad, perhaps to document what she'd seen. She smiled as she began to write using her special calligraphy pen, standing there in the street like an artist or a photographer. She loved her craft and although I hadn't read her work yet, I felt it must be good, despite all our differences. She understood pleasure and made room for it in her life.

Suddenly, I felt a sharp pang of jealousy. Not toward Natasha, but toward the couple, of their freedom. I wanted to hang up the telephone and be next to her. Kiss her on the eyes. Share in her pleasure as the couple shared in each other's.

If I were alone, my travels would have been much different.

Natasha wouldn't spend much time in museums. She had devoted a total of forty-five minutes to the Louvre, half of which was spent in line to see the *Mona Lisa*. The flocks of tourists clustered about this image did little to pique my interest, although Natasha, like the others, seemed to be impressed by ubiquitous images that were already popular, a much easier route than discovering beauty on her own. The painting was underwhelming to me. Perhaps because the image was common—a face I nearly recognized as my own—common, plain, and almost prudish. I had no idea what the world saw in the woman.

"That's all I wanted to see," Natasha said, ready for something new. The idea of leaving the Louvre so soon seemed sacrilegious. I simply couldn't. People flew into Paris and bought weeklong passes for the Louvre, never seeing enough. We agreed to split up for the afternoon, and meet back at the museum fountain.

The afternoon, however, was anticlimactic. I stood in front of some of the most sought-after pieces of art in the world—Ingres's *Turkish Bath,* sensual and exotic, and Rembrandt's life-size nude of Bathsheba bathing, a rich layering of ochre paints and white light. There was J. W. Waterhouse, whose images I had never taken much notice of, as his work seemed a bit fantastic to me, rosy-cheeked nymphs languishing amongst lily pads. Yet, looking at them now, I thought of nothing but Natasha—where she might be, what she was doing. I imagined her sitting in a canoe, floating down the Seine, draped in crimson ruffles, her long nymph-like red hair spilling down her back, like one of Waterhouse's female figures, and holding a glass of port wine as she gazed at a male stranger on the shore.

I found myself checking my watch continuously that afternoon. I wandered into the Egyptian antiquities wing and finally found some solace in a Diorite statuette of Isis, along with a bronze statuette of Karomama, inlaid in gold and silver, perhaps believing that it was what Natasha would have liked. Her presence in my life now distracted me. Made me feel like a stranger to myself.

After the Egyptian exhibits, I browsed the gift shop and purchased a replica of a silver Egyptian-styled bracelet, spiral and coiled. It was copied from the Greco-Roman period, with decorative snake eyes, intended to ensure protection. Mother would have considered the purchase "frivolous," since it wasn't inexpensive and had no resale value, not being a brand name. Despite this, it felt really good to buy it, and it was a reminder of Natasha. How new it was to take pleasure in a gift of remembrance. I had the sales clerk clip the tag so that I could wear it immediately.

When we finally reunited, Natasha offered excuses for having not been able to stay with me at the Louvre, complaining of a headache and disliking the temperature inside the museum—it had apparently been "too chilly." She sat with me on the bench along the large pyramid fountain and lit a cigarette.

"I'm really addicted to these damn things. They should allow smoking in the Louvre. I just can't go more than a half hour without starting to really *jones*."

I told her about the Egyptian exhibit, the statues and wood paintings of pharaohs, ankhs, and symbols, and showed her my bracelet.

"Oh, my," she said, unclasping it from my wrist and placing it on hers. She slid it way up high, adjusting it to fit around the thickest section of her arm. "You're supposed to wear it like this. Like Cleopatra."

Seated beneath the dramatic architecture behind her, the great modern fountain and puffy white clouds overhead, Natasha seemed to blend perfectly into her surroundings. She looked like she belonged. I took a shot of her there, her knapsack swung over her shoulder, wisps of hair in her face, and standing tall, chest out. She seemed suddenly moved by the

Louvre, now that we were outside of it. It was exteriors, I think, that impressed her most.

"Why are you so patient with me?" she asked.

"I had a hard time trying to be patient at first," I confessed, "but then you started to grow on me. You have that effect, you know."

"Usually it's the other way around; people adore me and then they tire of me." She smiled. "I hope my knight has some of your qualities."

We were both rather tired and retreated to a cinema for a rest. To our surprise, there were no other guests in the theater. A dark, Portuguese film about death called *Requiem* was playing, subtitled in French. I understood almost all of it, which surprised me a little. I had apparently absorbed more in my high school classes than I had imagined, although I couldn't decide if the protagonist was a man or a woman. There seemed to be no love interest, just a protagonist in a dark overcoat trying to cope with the death of his or her father, who had been murdered. In the process of gathering the pieces of the crime, he (or she) discovered a subconscious realm of pain and unresolved traumas.

Natasha tried to follow the subtitles, translating a few of the sentences for me. Her breath was sweet from cinnamon candy. I wanted to get closer, to hold her hand again. I whispered, "Would you like me to massage your hand?"

Her whole arm was tense, so using both hands, I twisted her skin in opposing directions, working to relax the muscles and wring out some of the tension.

"Feels so nice," she said.

I agreed.

Just then, a man in a blue jacket that was much too small for his frame entered the theater and sat two seats down from us, in the same row. Of all the empty seats he could have chosen, he sat near us. I looked over at him, but he lowered his head when I did this, obviously not wanting to make eye contact.

Natasha said "your turn" and began to rub my shoulders while I, leaning forward in my seat, watched the screen that showed overexposed black and white shots of the man or woman, still searching for someone they knew to be dead. Natasha's fingertips felt soft against the top of my back. I hadn't washed my shirt in a few days and the neck had stretched, exposing my skin. Natasha pressed a handful of long fingernails down the front of my shirt. I whispered to her how good it felt, only to hear labored breathing coming from the man two seats down. His breathing increased until we both looked over. He was furiously masturbating while giving us a glassy-eyed look. Natasha said to the man sternly, one eyebrow raised, *"Pardon!"*

He jumped and ran from the theater, the spell now broken. Natasha and I would have to start again, some other way.

The Moulin Rouge, on the Boulevard de Clichy. A side of town where the windmill vane rotated above the rooftop. We found a salon of mirrored walls, round glass globe lamps on every table, and topless cancan dancers. The place looked half empty, but the show still went on. It was not the old world experience I had anticipated, but something more closely resembling an opening act one would find in Las Vegas: stiff and uncreative, overly rehearsed and utterly lacking in sincerity. The ballroom smelled musty, of tobacco and sweat, the modern red carpets worn and faded to a lighter hue. The dancers weren't that pretty, and all of them seemed to be in their late thirties to early forties, heavily made up with dark rouge and eyeliner. Everywhere, breasts were sagging. The music was overly sensational, like something from a cheap carnival—perpetual climax. Despite all of this, Natasha was beaming with excitement. She'd strongly anticipated this event and had saved for the admission which was shockingly high for what it was. But she appreciated, I imagined, its Vegas-like commercialism. We ordered champagne and toasted each other, our glasses clinking.

"*A tes amours.*"

"*A tes amours,*" I echoed.

Cigarette girls walked throughout the labyrinth of tables carrying boxes of tobacco, mints, and bubble gum, wearing tights and leotards, winking at no one in particular. "Cigar? Cigarette? Cigar? Cigarette?" they chirped.

The girls' accents were charming. Natasha and I turned to each other and grinned.

But it was when Natasha was pulled onto the stage by the show master for a Chaplin-esque routine that my spirits for the evening began to shift. Witnessing her going through the motions on stage, all smiles and blushes, getting teased and chased by the host and liking the attention of it all, I understood just how different we were, and how even at my most confident, I would never care so much for other people as she did. How wonderful it must have felt to be the one to have baited her smile. I instantly recalled the times her smile had been aimed at me, such as the moment she'd found me waiting for her at the airport gate, or the photo session we'd had in the gondola, and the time I'd tried the trick of raising one brow. I realized how important this was to her—how she seemed to depend on others to bring her fulfillment, which took trust and faith in the outside world—and I envied that more than anything. I decided, watching her smile grow wider, her skin flushing pink with heat, that I was in love with her.

I felt as if we were a couple on holiday now, playing all the silly tourist games, using up time—days—as though they were just an empty space to fill until the moments that came later, when real conversations and private emotions would happen back in the hotel room, when all was stillness. I pictured the room, like a photograph, the simple furnishings and sunlight coming in from the street through the balcony windows, toothbrushes next to one another on the sink, and the floral scent of Natasha's towels after one of her nightly showers. I longed for this stillness.

A fear of sorts had left my body while watching the show, and something else had taken its place—something larger than myself. The mystery was no longer enough to sustain me—I needed to know her intimately.

In the Moulin Rouge gift shop, Natasha purchased a cassette tape of the show's theme music. Although not interested in any mementos from the night, I discovered the miniature reproduction posters of Toulouse-Lautrec's, including one of my favorite dancers from the turn of the century: Jane Avril, her famous "snake dress" winding tight around her torso, mouth in a pout of both pleasure and pain. I read on the back of the poster that she had never even owned a "snake dress," that it was an invention of Lautrec's meant to complement Jane's snake-like style of dancing. I purchased the print and gave it to Natasha. She handed over the cassette in return and I blushed appreciatively.

Tired, Natasha and I decided to take a taxi back to our room, which we were already calling "home."

"Hotel du Progres," Natasha directed to the driver. "Latin Quarter."

The taxi driver didn't seem to understand the directions,

but nevertheless continued to drive. He was weaving in and out of other cars, thick glasses flopping on a chain around his neck as he belched.

"You look like you're on honeymoon," the cab driver said to us, in a heavy French accent.

We giggled and whispered, deciding that the driver was confused in his translations.

The following morning Natasha decided to wear her mother's wedding dress, which smelled slightly of mothballs. I was becoming impatient. The chemistry between us was evident, and neither of us was brave enough to make a pass.

"It's just an old hippie gown," she said, trying to downplay its symbolic role. It was cream-colored and lacy and fit her perfectly. She doused on essential oils to help cover the mothball scent.

"Was your mother a virgin when she wore that?" I asked.

"Fuck, no," she said, dabbing oil behind each ear. "Are you kidding? She listened to Janis Joplin, dropped acid, and messed around in orgies like the rest of them." Natasha painted on a berry-stained lipstick and hooked delicate silver earrings into her earlobes. Tiny moons dangled from each hoop. "Let's be crazy today," she said. "Fuck tourism. Fuck the Moulin Rouge."

She seemed to have read my mind. "Let's get fucked up," I said.

Still wearing my uniform-like clothing—Capri pants and a long white oxford tied in the front—I, too, longed for another option. My shapelessly styled hair seemed like a hindrance now. Who was I underneath all this? I was someone else—this I was sure of. I wanted to find this new woman.

I stepped out onto our tiny veranda and stretched my arms out to the street. The cool morning air woke my senses and made me feel naked, even though I wasn't. But I felt free. Perhaps it was because our room was so high, and I could see everything that lay before me. Above the mass of bustling cars and busy pedestrians, I was separated from the pressure of the earth's labors, positioned in a place that couldn't exhaust, and only replenished. Like a great ocean bluff, I was no longer vulnerable to the daily tides of the streets. I felt in charge of my day.

"I want to do something radical!" I shouted.

We found a hair salon, nearly empty, and I had my hair cut into a French-style bob. I now looked like a light-haired Egyptian, my face angular and defined. I looked in the mirror and experienced the satisfaction of seeing an image that reflected what I felt inside: intense. Why hadn't I done this long ago?

Natasha said she was trying to grow her hair out and decided to just have hers washed and dried. She wouldn't let me pay her tab. At the counter, as we were pulling out our money, I noticed that she was looking at me differently than before.

When Natasha caught my gaze, it took her a moment to find words. "You've changed," she said bashfully, curling her mouth inward, like a child's. She playfully flitted her fingers through the hair that curled around my ear. "This suits you much better."

We stopped at a small café for a carafe of Bordeaux, sitting out on the patio so that we could watch people passing by. There was recorded music coming from a square up ahead—it sounded like Madonna. Feeling something pulling me, I gulped down my glass of wine, encouraging Natasha to do the same. I grabbed her hand and left a large bill on the table for the wine.

"Come on," I said.

When we arrived at the square, we came up on a crowd of about sixty spectators watching a man lip-sync to a Madonna song that was blaring from a cheap, but large, radio. He wasn't good at all, or even that funny, so I decided to show him something.

"Could you hold onto this for me?" I asked Natasha, handing her my small leather backpack and camera.

"Sure," she said hesitantly. "What are you going to do?"

Without answering her, I ran into the center of the square, where the man was dancing. When he saw me coming, he stepped aside, allowing me to take the stage. I began to lip-sync to the song *Lucky Star* and dance along to the music, mimicking a Madonna video I had seen on MTV. Nothing about what I was doing was me—which was precisely the thrill. That a crowd had mistaken this lively person for me fed a hunger that I hadn't kown I had until a few days ago.

How many times would I have to do something as silly—as impulsive—to rid myself of the person I had left home?

I brought my hands over my head, swiveling my hips around. The crowd cheered, much more so than they had for the man. This obviously didn't please him, as he began waving his hands at me to go away. I bowed to the audience and returned to Natasha, who was quietly waiting, standing there in her mother's old wedding dress, beaming like a proud parent.

We raced through an alley, away from the crowd. Our new hair flying behind us, we ran hand in hand toward our next destination: the Eiffel Tower. Some French boys approached us, trying to initiate a conversation in their broken English, "I love *vous*," they tried. Natasha put her arm around my shoulder as we jogged on. I felt that she was claiming me as her own, her nurturing arm holding me tight, ready to protect me.

I felt an erotic charge surge through me. *"Ma femme,"* she hollered back over her shoulder to the boys. *My wife.* The boys laughed and pointed, and I mashed a big kiss on her cheek, just to emphasize the point. I didn't bother to look for their reactions. Natasha's cheek was as soft as a child's and as we touched, she gripped my back a little tighter. We continued on our way.

I could barely feel my feet.

The Eiffel Tower stands nine hundred and eighty-six feet high. At its base, we read the plaques describing the details of the immense metal structure and its history. During the building stages, some of the locals had feared the tower would alter weather patterns. Many people didn't trust its safety, but the foundations were and still are state-of-the-art, sunk deeply into the clay of the earth and inserted at an angle to provide further stability. When it was first built, Parisians had been afraid that it would destroy the beauty of the Paris skyline. Critics had asked Gustav Eiffel, the architect of the tower, if he thought that engineers could create beautiful structures at all, and Eiffel replied, "Is it because we are engineers that we do not pay attention to beauty? Do not the laws of natural forces always conform to the secret laws of harmony?" And with time, the tower had come to symbolize Paris.

"What does it mean to you?" Natasha asked, her head tilted, gazing up towards its tip. "It looks phallic to me," she said before I could respond.

I looked up at the monument, its vaulted roof structures, a great skeleton of bridges, decks, and various other supports. In some ways, it seemed like the Western answer to the Egyptian Pyramids, in its almost unattainable precision.

"Freedom," I answered.

★   ★   ★

I phoned Mother from Altitude 95, the restaurant on the first floor of the tower, its namesake a reference to its location at ninety-five meters above sea level. I was afraid to continue to the top.

The phone rang and rang, until I heard the line cut out and looked up to see that Natasha had pressed her finger down on the pay phone's receiver.

"Why did you do that?"

"Are you kidding?" she said. "You can't call your mom from the Eiffel Tower. I just won't allow it. If you can't do this without her, it won't count. Just get drunk."

I set the receiver back down, aware that the sound of Mother's voice might actually deter me from climbing the tower.

Large bay windows framed the restaurant's three hundred sixty degree view, which overlooked the Seine, the Trocadero, and the interior of the tower. Natasha and I walked over to the bar, all chrome and mirrors. I didn't see my reflection this time, but rather the image of a man. I turned and spotted a painter, strapped and harnessed to one of the girders, a tool belt and paint bucket hanging from his sides. My stomach dropped just imagining how he must have felt, dangling over the city, vulnerable, with nothing but a rope and straps to depend on. He was painting the tower its signature reddish-brown color, his body spattered from head to boots in the paint.

"You already made it this far," Natasha said as she rested a hand on my shoulder. "Might as well see it all."

After three glasses of dry champagne, we rode the elevators to the top.

Natasha lit two cigarettes and handed me one.

At the peak of the tower, Paris appeared still and peaceful. The silhouettes cast by people on the ground made them appear like tiny black dots of ink on the streets. I felt euphoric, as though I were on the top of a great mountain, my head light and dreamy.

"I wish we could go higher," I said.

Below, the rest of the world seemed to be sinking farther beneath us.

"One young man tried," Natasha said, closing her eyes and sucking a long drag from her cigarette. "He'd worked the full two-year duration constructing the tower, then upon its completion, flung himself over the edge as his girlfriend watched below. I read about it on a plaque at the base. The city still speculates about the meaning of his death."

"I suppose suicide could be an act of freedom," I said, glancing down through the safety bars at the city below. All the alcohol had made me dizzy. I'd forgotten about the wine we'd had earlier, which was totaling up to one fantastic slur. "We control our pleasures, so, hey, why not control our pain?"

Natasha dropped her cigarette over the edge, and blowing smoke from her lips, leaned into me.

I kissed her back, my lips parting slightly—enough, that is, to feel her full lips and tongue pressing into me as if to say, "yes." It was my first caress of a woman, and was not unlike the first time I had ever descended beneath water—something I greatly feared, yet once I leapt in, it came as naturally, it seemed, as breathing.

I just had to remember to come up for air.

Back at our pension, we rode the narrow elevator up to our room. It was an ancient contraption with a black-gated

door and only room enough for two. When we had first arrived, we had to take the elevator up one at a time, since we
were carrying luggage. Colored walls passed as we ascended
through floors of brightly-lit corridors, dark pillars, and rails
alternately casting striped shadows across our bodies, now
pressed together tightly in the confined space. We could hear
each other's breath, our chests rising against one another in
the tight space as we breathed.

Our room had a simple beauty—a Bohemian minimal-
ism. There was a table and two chairs. A mirrored armoire. A
vase containing a single carnation. Two unframed beds: the
double and the very insignificant-looking French single we
had both avoided.

I undressed to the sounds of Natasha brushing her teeth
in the tiny bathroom. I slid into the cool bleached sheets of
the larger bed, my feet pressing into the tightly tucked cotton,
my heart pounding. The aroma of alcohol lingered throughout
the room. I had never felt so impatient in all my life.

Natasha pulled her dress over her shoulders and slid into
bed with me, the scent of her breath minty as she found a
comfortable position and covered herself with the sheet.

I wasn't tired, and the evening sunset filled the room with
enough light to make me realize how early it must have still
been. I lay on my side, studying Natasha's face. As always, her
expression was warm and open, like the sun. Eyes relaxed, lids
heavy and glad, nearly closed. A little smirk rose from the corner of her mouth. I took a deep breath and rolled onto her
body.

She giggled and closed her eyes completely, tilting her
head back, inviting my lips. I came at her, into her neck, tasting the sandalwood fragrance of her skin.

My jaw stiffened at the thought of her submissiveness, as

though her body were entirely at my disposal for pleasure. I wondered if this was how men might have felt with women much of the time.

My lips traveled down her delicate throat until I reached the soft ridge between her full breasts. Grazing her nipples required more bravery, but I released my tongue, swirling around the rosy outlines. Each second felt like an eternity as my heart hammered in fear of her sudden rejection. She began to take heavy breaths and placed her hands on either side of my face.

My head fell lower to her small waist and warm belly, then bravely along the line of her panties. For a brief moment, I wondered if I was moving too fast, and if, perhaps, I should have asked her permission. But I could not stop my fingers, which found their way inside the material and felt the small web of hair—a coarseness that made my body twinge and stir. There was no going back.

I caressed her softly, rubbing across the hair and lifting her panties enough to see that blessed auburn, the color of her true hair, which I had taken only a glimpse of in Amsterdam. Now it was mine to not just see, but to touch. I pulled her panties to one side and began to rub with my palm and then nestled my tongue in deep, where it was hard like a bone, and slowly licked back and forth as she breathed even heavier, crying out a little. It was all happening so fast, my hands and lips on her body, and I couldn't stop it.

"Please!" she begged, only I wasn't exactly sure what she wanted.

Her body wiggled as I rolled her panties down and pulled one of her feet out, so that the material was left to dangle against her pale thigh. I ran my hands along her smoothly shaved skin, trying to make the moment last, reveling in her sweet, peach-vanilla taste. I kept trying to sustain this moment like a recording that I was going to try to replay again and again. I wanted to get the most out of each touch, and let each moment burn itself into a memory that I could savor long afterwards.

Her sex became dominant, like the crest of a tiny wave. I set her in my mouth. The more I rolled my tongue around, the harder she got.

She arched her back, letting out a gasp as I softly placed a finger inside of her as well, her body convulsing and tightening around it.

"You feel too good," she said, gripping my shoulders and rocking back and forth. She squeezed tighter as I went farther in, until my finger was in as deeply as possible. Her wetness intensified.

Her body drew back from my lips. "No fair," she said. "My turn now."

She pushed me off her until I fell back onto the bed. I waited desperately for her touch to come, wondering how it would feel, and what part of my body she wanted to explore first.

Starting with my lips, she began to tour her way down my body with light kisses, her soft red hair brushing my face, neck, and breasts, her hair so wild that I couldn't see her face at all. She kissed my stomach, her hands and lips softer than anything I'd ever felt against my skin. She slid in between my legs and spread them wide, lowering her face and licking low and deep like a cat at its paws. I stretched my legs out even farther and moaned.

Time and space became meaningless within a new world of surreal warmth. At one point, I brought my thighs up over her shoulders and pressed the back of my heels against her smooth back. Her tongue seemed to widen inside me until I let out a cry of pleasure. She seemed to know exactly what my body wanted. She finally threw her bright red mass of curls behind her to make eye contact with me again. Her eyes looked nearly demonic, like she was possessed by a spirit much more ruthless than I'd known.

My past with men was suddenly reduced to a single flash. All encounters before had been practice, nothing more. And none of it had prepared me for the pleasure I was finding here. I dug my nails deep into her flesh, angered that she had kept me waiting for this for so long. From now on, I knew I would have to look outside of myself for my happiness.

"Natasha!" I cried out into the silence of the room, not caring whether anyone else could hear me.

I arched my back higher, until she finally collapsed onto my body, this time our mouths colliding, the taste of our scents mixing as our tongues wrestled—cat hungry.

A silent choreography existed between us. We knew what would happen next. I wrapped my arms around her back and turned her over until I was on top of her, smashing my body against hers. We began to rub, our legs locked together, rotating our hips, our bodies becoming slick and wet, our sexes spread flat against one another's, as though pressing against windows. Consumed with the desire to envelop each other, we moved up and down like a man and woman would. The small penetration our bodies were able to find with one another seemed just enough to make us want more, and within moments we were gliding fast. I could feel her heart thundering against my breasts as we shook, my head becoming so light until we both came, squeezing until every last ounce of strength had been wrung from our bodies. With this, we seemed to have reached one irrefutable truth.

Natasha lunged her wet tongue down my throat, the tongue that had been inside me for the last half hour. Being with her felt honest and justified. With men it had been different—no need this time for a vigorous shower afterwards to get my insides back, or the questioning of whether or not I had "given in." Back home I'd stuck things out with Grant, it seemed, just to make me look better, as though trying to build some type of résumé. What I had found with Natasha was no simple "experience." I no longer cared about how my life looked on paper. The old rules no longer applied.

The last bit of daylight fell onto the bed, making our skin look yellow. I liked the way it played against our bodies, producing shadows across us, giving the appearance of leopard spots. Natasha rested her face in the crook of my neck. As we listened to each other's breathing, our hands ran against one another's backs which, for some reason, made me think of being at the beach—rubbing, warming her smooth skin, inhaling its sweet scents, transporting me to salt and body oils, sunning in white sand.

"Think you'll ever find your knight?" I asked, looking down at our bodies. Our figures differed greatly, and I couldn't help comparing hers to mine—mine appearing almost masculine next to hers, so thin, producing more shadows along my kneecaps and hipbones and amongst the small muscles of my stomach—while she looked like a goddess.

"I made my wish," she said, reaching up to run her fingers through my tousled hair. Her eyes blinked sleepily as she sat up on one elbow and lit a cigarette, offering me one.

"No, thanks," I said. I let several seconds pass. "I couldn't possibly feel any better than I do right now."

"Yeah. That was the best I've ever had," she said, pausing. "With a woman."

I hated that she'd put it that way, hated what it said about who I wasn't, and what I'd been unable to provide, an idea that for me seemed limitless.

"We can do anything," I said, the words liberating me even more as soon as they left my lips. "Nothing we do has to be predictable. What do men have that we don't!"

"Armor," she said strangely, stabbing out her cigarette and folding her body back inwards against me, spine curled outward, stomach relaxed and overlapping, my thoughts once again connecting her to one of the voluptuous Waterhouse figures—unconsciously seductive, lips parted as she breathed. Her hair loose and fiery.

All I could think of was how good it would feel to make love to her again.

Chapter 7

Delilah Blue

I woke the next morning to a cold bed and the sounds of vomiting. Natasha's body was no longer next to mine. She was sick, and for a moment, I let myself think it was because of me, of what I had done with her last night.

I closed my eyes and forced myself back to sleep.

When I woke later, she was sitting on the other small bed, painting her nails purple. Her mother's white dress lay across the mattress, alongside her like a ghost.

"Are you okay?"

"I'll live," she said, shrugging her shoulders.

"How long have you been awake?" I yawned, trying my best to remain relaxed. I was afraid things had changed between us.

Natasha picked up her hand, observed her fingers closely, and blew on them to try to dry the polish. "I slept like shit," she said, not bothering to look up at me. "I never sleep well when I drink."

That was the first time that day that she would call attention to having drunk so much. There would be more. I felt as though she was making it unmistakably clear that her partic-

ipation in last night's affair had been because of the alcohol
and that it had been a mistake. At a nearby café, we were going
to order a brunch of eggs, croissants, and juice, but at the last
moment she changed her mind.

"You know what I'd like more than anything else in the
world right now?" she asked.

"Armor?"

"McDonald's French fries. Did you see the yellow arches
on our way to the Metro?"

"I must have missed it."

She told the waiter we'd changed our minds.

We ended up having to ride the Metro back to the
McDonald's, the subway packed with nine-to-fivers making
their way to work. I inhaled a deep breath, my hand on one
of the rails for support, thinking how awkward it would be to
have to be so close to strangers all the time, first thing in the
morning like this.

When the subway reached our destination, Natasha and I
quickly exited first and I turned to take a few shots of the
commuters coming up the ramp. One man dressed in business attire raised his left hand to cover his face as he walked,
wanting to remain indistinguishable from the mass of other
commuters.

"Rude," Natasha said, glancing back at me as I released
the shutter.

I didn't dare ask her what she meant by this. I decided
that she was probably right and that the photos were point-
less.

Paris McDonald's: not unlike a strip club or a rave.
William Orbit playing through speakers overhead. Smells of
patchouli and French fries filled the air. Disco lights flashed,

or was it just a microwave door opening? The cashiers had multiple facial piercings, fluorescent hair, and platform sneakers beneath their black uniform pants. One employee ground her hips to the music, while mopping up spilled catsup.

Two girls, one American, one Japanese, were quarrelling near the register. The Japanese girl picked her camera up off the floor, crying. "Why travel without camera? How will they know I've been to Paris?" She had clean brown hair, the top section highlighted and clipped back into a barrette. She was wearing tight white pants and a tank top that said "Gucci" across the front in red letters.

At the condiment stand, a boy with spiked hair stirred cream into his coffee and told us that he was an American making his way across Europe on a McDonald's tour, logging it all in his journal. He shared the journal with us and when he opened it, the smell beneath his arms revealed that he hadn't showered in days. His eyes gaped up at us hungrily, then back at his book filled with labels and stickers and collage art, then back up at our shirts.

"Would you look at my chest when I'm talking to you!" Natasha said sarcastically as she got up and walked away.

Over coffee and fries, I suggested we share last night's dreams.

"I dreamed of a beautiful woman with perfect breasts, a huge penis, and a long, flapping tail," she said, dipping a wad of fries into a puddle of catsup and stuffing them into her mouth.

I wondered what the woman represented: Natasha, myself, or something deeper, perhaps an ideal? The idea that a woman who could possess the qualities of both sexes and wear both genitalia beautifully stretched my brain.

"Alcohol makes me have weird dreams," she said, taking a sip of her coffee and peeking up at me, as though waiting for my turn to share. She wasn't wearing any makeup, and she looked tired and drained in the harsh daylight coming in through the windows. She was a different person.

I wondered if I had done this to her, robbed her of her vivacity and color by having made love to her and enjoying her with such selfish pleasure. I wondered, too, if when she looked at me, if my looks had changed as well, if I seemed as unfamiliar to her as she did to me.

I was afraid to tell her of my dream. I picked up the shaker of salt and began to over-salt my fries so that I wouldn't have to look at her when I told her. My stomach ached with an emptiness I couldn't feed.

"I dreamed of a dog. It was pink and bald, like a pig, with black spiky hairs around her head," I explained. She was silent, so I continued to explain even more, wanting to make it sound as appealing as possible. "In the dream, I was supposed to adopt the dog because it was pregnant and needed a home. It had big maternal eyes that made me sick with guilt."

What I didn't explain, but what seemed so obvious to me, was what the creature represented—the beast that was awakened last night in our bed, something which frightened and humiliated me.

"Weird," she commented, taking another sip of her coffee, her face directed out towards the windows. She put her hand over her mouth and ran to the bathroom.

When she returned, she repeated how she should never drink so much. I finished my fries and coffee, and eyed my bare napkin, the layer of salt left there. I began to absently rake it together into a little pile with my finger, wondering how I would make it through the day.

★ ★ ★

Walking along the Seine, passing the Hotel De Ville. Café boats floating, couples everywhere. Lovers dangling their plump legs over the river walls, breaking baguettes, sharing bottles of Bordeaux. Couples kissing and snuggling beneath wool blankets, necks and arms outstretching towards one another.

Natasha had begun to ignore me again, just as she had done at the beginning of our trip. My suggestions as to what we might do next, or comments on the landscape, meant little to her. I was hungry again, but Natasha wasn't interested in stopping at another café. I trailed behind her, carrying the map, searching for the famous bookstore we had planned on finding, searching for my lucky star.

I felt more alone than ever and was slightly homesick— But what did I have to return to? I couldn't even remember.

It was a bright cool day, reminiscent of spring. The way beginnings should feel, although today was turning out to seem more like an ending. Watching the couples, I couldn't help but wonder if mutual love was truly possible, or if it was merely a state of delusion for one, if not both, of the lovers. There seemed to exist a promise of forever in romance that reality defied.

If only love were rare, I thought—less often experienced—an emotion that occurred infrequently enough that it could be compared to times when love was absent. What if love were an emotion so strong that the only thing one could compare it to was the yawning emptiness of being alone? In this way, when love finally happened to two people, it would change their lives forever.

Love seemed like photography for me—yet another thing that people took advantage of, not letting it say what it wanted to say. An expression often limited by the perceiver.

I took the cap off the camera lens, slid the F-stop up two notches, and aimed it at Natasha, hoping she might warm up to what had originally brought us together.

"Do you mind?" she said and glared at me.

It was so humiliating that I took the camera and aimed it at the landscape filled with other couples. I didn't even care who or what I was aiming at. I took advantage of the mass of everything around me, relieved to hide behind the lens as I took the photo.

"Don't be fooled by the foreigners," Natasha said, turning away from the river and back toward the bridge where the taxis waited. She still wouldn't look at me. "They have problems just like everyone else."

"That's what I'm photographing," I said quickly, without thinking. "The problems."

The place looked dead. There was no sign, no lights, and the door was boarded over. We checked the address in Natasha's *Let's Go* economy travel guide, to make sure we were at the right building.

"This can't be it," Natasha said, checking her guidebook a third time.

We had found Shakespeare and Co., the famous bookstore owned by Sylvia Beach, the meeting place for many influential writers of the twenties and thirties.

"I can't believe Anaïs Nin and Hemingway and Gertrude Stein spent their time here. Here! And then someone just closes it up."

There was graffiti sprayed on the outside of the door—names and paper signs advertising music shows were taped to the boarded-up windows. My reflection in the abandoned shop window startled me. I felt instantly confident at my new streamlined look, grew taller and smiled. I kept forgetting my appearance had been altered so much by the haircut.

Before we left the remains of Shakespeare and Co., Natasha took out her pad and wrote a few lines with her calligraphy pen, then closed the book and began walking towards the alley where we'd come from. "I hate it when people give up on a dream," she said. "I hate Paris. They should have made it last."

"Maybe they just closed for a remodel?"

"Fuck this shit. Europe sucks and it's too expensive. Do you realize that yesterday I spent the equivalent of thirty dollars at the grocery store on a bottle of water, a yogurt, a pack of cigarettes, a bag of nuts, and two bananas? They charged us for use of the shopping cart, and at the checkout counter we had to pay extra for the paper bags to carry them out in. And I have never in my life had so much trouble finding a bathroom in a city. Why won't shopkeepers let us use their rest rooms? I don't get it. I'm going to write my own travel guide for Europe," she finished. "I'm going to call it *Let's Leave.*"

Standing outside the train platform, waiting to depart from Paris, I phoned my mother using the phone card she'd given me before I left. She'd made me promise to call her at least three times a week and lately I hadn't.

"It's been almost a week. What happened? I've been worried. I thought you must have died."

She uttered these words with such ease it filled me with horror. I imagined her response had I actually died—nothing more than a frustration?

"What if I had?" I asked. "Would you come get my body

or have me shipped back home on my own? After all, you haven't taken a vacation for a while."

She let out a long huff. "Sometimes, Danielle, your humor is beyond me."

"Sometimes things do happen for a reason."

"I don't believe that," she said. "People make mistakes all the time, but just don't have the courage to admit it to themselves."

"I drank too much last night," I said.

There was a pause. "I don't trust Paris," she said. "Not unless it's done in a group, some sort of tour. You must make a tight agenda and stick to it, so you don't waste your time."

It disgusted me how she referred to the act of traveling as "doing."

"Paris isn't an activity, a sport, or a game, Mother, but a real place filled with real people living their lives!"

Mother began to chuckle knowingly. "Well then, did you fall in love with a *real* man?"

I didn't want to answer her, or speak to her anymore. It was so clear that she really didn't care about me or my journey. All she cared about was how closely I was fitting into her agenda of who she wanted me to be, and what she wanted me to be doing. I felt like a little doll, propped into place and spoken for.

I took a deep breath and told her that I hadn't fallen in love.

She smacked her lips and paused. "Well, the boys here will be glad to know this." Her words came out high-pitched and phony, as when she spoke to female neighbors or members of her clubs on the telephone.

"Grant called. He sends his regards and wants to take you out again when you return," she went on. "I think you should give him a call while you're over there, just to let him know you're still interested, so he won't forget you. Use my calling card."

"I didn't bring his number."

"How well your mother knows you! I figured you'd forgotten it so I asked him for it this morning when he called. Got a pen?"

I searched for a pen in my backpack while Mother continued to chat. I couldn't see Natasha. She had probably stepped outside the depot, or slipped inside one of the cafés.

"Sometimes I feel so bad for the men you bring around. You are so fickle. Men have pride, you know."

"What about women?" I asked sharply.

"What about them?"

"Don't we have pride?"

She laughed. "Well, you certainly don't."

My forehead pressed against the cool glass window of the train, I watched landscape travel backwards. I realized, too, that I had forgotten my journal in the Paris pension. I hadn't written in it since Greece, so I felt I'd lost nothing.

I was tired and longed for the solace of my bedroom, if just for twelve hours. A bath. A tall glass of Ovaltine. Enough to replenish my energy and get my wits back. I craved isolation now, and thought of my life back home—the long quiet days of routine, waking to my alarm, dressing, getting a bagel at the campus café, time spent alone in the darkroom. The darkroom was a place where I could forget everything—a place that could absorb anything in its silence and darkness, the smell of chemicals fermenting, preserving a moment that in the real world could never last. But what was the point now

that I knew I was no photographer? I had lost faith in yet another home. What comfort was left but in the cold steel
tracking before me, leading me to yet another foreign place.

I had wrapped myself in magazines and images. I'd grown
so accustomed to the isolation of my life that I had built up
little immunity to the effects that others had upon me. My
lack of resistance to others seemed to be magnified now that
I had no place to escape to—no bedroom, no darkroom in
which I could simply close the door and shut out everything.
These places were luxuries I no longer believed I deserved.
I'd been so rude to Mother, and I was no photographer.

At a layover, we debarked the train for a shopping break.
We found a secondhand shop near the station and tried on
shirts.

Natasha purchased a polyester disco top in a color she
called "Delilah Blue." She was thrilled. "Perfect for Prague."

"I look like a dyke," I said, standing before a mirror in a
white crew neck blouse, afraid I hadn't met Natasha's expectations.

Did true romance have to involve fear? Was this what had
been missing from my life, this longing for another paired
with this obsession over whether or not someone felt the
same for me as I for them? Somehow, perhaps due to a lack of
experience, I didn't feel entitled to my feelings towards
Natasha—that I hadn't earned them. After all, I wasn't a man.

Natasha didn't hear me, or perhaps she chose not to respond to the comment, urging me instead to make up my
mind before we missed the train.

I decided that I liked nothing and told her I'd meet her
back on the train, that I wanted to do a bit more shopping on
my own.

I walked the cobblestone streets, searching for a gift for
Mother. It seemed suddenly important that I find her a sou-

venir, and that it was she who deserved to be tended to. Many
of the shops were closed already, even though it was still light.
I darted into a record store and asked where I might find a
souvenir shop, and I was directed, in very broken English,
down an alleyway that was said to be a good place for tourists.

The alleyway was gray and tunneled, shadowed from the
sun, and there were no commercial shops in sight. I checked
my watch and saw that the train would be departing in just
ten minutes, and although I should have turned around, I felt
compelled to return to the train with a gift for Mother. I
thought about everything she had stuffed into my travel pack
before I left. With the exception of the romance novel, I had
used all of the other items: the two rolls of toilet paper, the
sanitary wipes, the antibacterial waterless soap, and the bed-
side flashlight for finding my way to the washroom at night. I
was struck with the need to pay her back for her efforts to
protect me.

I reached the end of the alley and turned right, no longer
looking for a souvenir shop, but any retail shop that would be
open. The street had now become a strip of office complexes,
flats, and then a bank. I looked back towards the direction I'd
come, and realized that I would have to turn around. It seemed
that tracing my steps would not be the best route to getting
back to the train, so I began to walk around the block, intuiting that I would soon reach the train station. Minutes passed,
however, and I saw no sign of the train station, and nothing
familiar.

I decided to try an alley this time, hoping that it would
lead to the other alleyway I'd crossed, and that I might recognize one of the shops or streets that veered from it. My
breathing had quickened and I couldn't draw a deep breath. I
began running. There were only a few minutes left before the
train departed. The train's doors might have been locking at

that very moment. I had no idea what I would do if I were left behind. I couldn't even recall the name of the town I was in. I'd become lost, and I longed for Mother more than ever.

And then I heard bells ringing. The sound was coming from the station, only about a block away. I ran in the direction of the ringing and then it was all there, the station, train, but the doors had already shut and all the passengers were back inside. The whistle blew. I started running toward the train.

I passed several train cars, trying to find car number three eleven, hoping that Natasha, at least, might see me and try and stop the train.

"Help," I yelled out to the passengers as I ran alongside the train, scanning the cars for anyone who was watching and who might hear me. "Stop the train!"

And then, bringing instant relief, the doors opened back up and I leaped inside. The doors closed behind me, the whistle blew, and the train started. I wasn't on car number three eleven, but I was on my train and I was safe.

None of the other passengers seemed to notice me, or to be aware of what I had just gone through. I walked down the aisles of the cars, passing men and women who didn't look up from their books or away from the sandwiches they were eating. They hadn't seen me running alongside the train. No one knew I had been lost or separated from my traveling companion. But why would they? They had their own concerns.

I tried to slow my pace so that I could begin to relax and catch my breath. My heart was still racing and I was perspiring beneath my arms and across my forehead, unable to calm down. I tried to tell myself that everything was fine now, that I had no more worries, and that my luggage and my locked camera and the stranger I was traveling with were worth returning to. But somehow, I couldn't hear myself.

* * *

Natasha wore headphones, listening to the compilation of songs she'd made for the trip: Tori Amos, Jewel, Ani DiFranco, and Sarah Brightman. She was wrapped in her own thoughts, defended against the outside world, seemingly unaware of my return or my fatigue. An old woman with thick, graying eyebrows looked both Natasha and me up and down, as if she knew what was going on between us.

I asked the woman if she knew how long it was to our next stop, Berlin.

"Six," she said, pointing to her watch. "I hope you brought blankets. It gets cold." I wasn't sure if she meant six hours or six A.M. . . . Either answer seemed like an eternity. I took more deep breaths and slipped off my sandals, trying to get ahold of my nerves.

There was a man seated in front of us exchanging jokes with two attractive British women. Some humor was just what I needed. His English was broken, but the story could still be made out, the punch lines found, and I realized that there was no language barrier when it came to laughter: "Woman stand in front of mirror, fondling . . . Is that how you say? Caress? Herself. 'I need a man,' she says, bringing her hair up off her shoulder and twisting her body. She had a son who was watching her through door creaked open." He paused long enough to clear his throat and gather his next words. "Okay. Later that day, boy sees, ah, mother in bed with man." His words came out choppy. "In the morning when man is gone and mother is out of bedroom, boy goes into mother's room and stand in front of mirror. Boy rubs his body and brings his hair up off his shoulders, caressing himself. 'I need a bicycle'."

I laughed along with the Englishwomen.

I looked back at Natasha, to see if she had heard the joke,

but she was only staring out the window, intently looking at nothing.

Ahead of us, near the end of our coach, was a young and attractive couple, patiently standing amid the tight, shifting crowd, waiting to be assigned to a coach. The man hung on a rail for support as the woman wrapped her arms around his waist, staring into his eyes. They spoke close and at one point, rubbed noses.

"I can't bear public affection," Natasha said, apparently more attentive than I'd realized.

The smell of sweet salami filled the car as Natasha began to pick at a cold sandwich she had brought along for the overnight ride. The woman who had questioned me earlier sat across from us now, removing her stockings. The bottoms of her feet revealed skin blackened with dirt and tar. She began to wash them with a bottle of water and a rag. The coach filled with a smell like rotting animals. I looked over to Natasha and she rolled her eyes in disgust at the sight.

Yesterday had been a rush of newness. I'd felt attractive and strong, unafraid to express my true feelings, and the love-making had just followed. Now on the train—overtired, wearing no makeup, and feeling bored, I didn't know if I would ever again be capable of being that confident person I had been yesterday. I began to feel myself slide back into the role of the girl who couldn't figure out why Natasha had ever been interested in me in the first place. Her disinterest in me now seemed to confirm this. I wished I knew how she felt about our encounter, what it was that I had done wrong.

We passed impressive cliffs through Germany, a sight which I barely blinked at, my mind in so many other places. Moving through tunnels, I would catch my own reflection in the window and it still managed to jar me. The changing lights fragmented the glimpses of my body, casting white diamonds of light upon my neck and chest.

Natasha looked gorgeous to me again in her denim cut-off shorts and low-cut tank top, cleavage almost always apparent. I preferred her this way: wearing basic clothes. She was enough of an enigma without costumes.

I flipped through a foreign magazine with disinterested speed. If only I had a way to think clearly and remain in the moment, or had a philosophy in which I could find solace, like Zen. I kept thinking about last night, about Natasha. If we only could have another chance. I finally made myself take some extra deep breaths and closed my eyes. Somehow, I fell asleep.

I dreamed of myself as sand in a windstorm, body separating into a thousand particles, all blown at great speed. I felt uncollected and light, moving in any direction I wished. I blew into the face of a woman, falling down her body to find her naked, pale, and embarrassed, her skin merging with me. I passed through the woman's body and she screamed, looking at me but not seeing my face, as I didn't have one. I wanted to tell her that everything was okay, that there was nothing to fear, but I didn't have a voice to say the words.

I awoke to the foot woman's belching and snoring, as though something was caught in her throat. The way her neck was bent appeared to be cutting off her breathing. I resisted the impulse to prop her up straight.

I was thirsty and out of water, and didn't want to ask Natasha to share from her bottle. I went to the washroom and drank a little from the faucet that had a sign with a cup and a line slashed through it, warning the passengers not to drink.

Natasha had her headset off and was looking out the window when I returned to my seat.

"Does what we did last night make you feel uncomfortable?" she asked, her eyes blinking without emotion. "Your behavior has changed."

"It was a mistake," I said. "I'm sorry."

Natasha raised her chin. She looked perplexed, the afternoon light coming in through the window, illuminating the small lines in her face. "You should ask people first," she said, glancing out at the passing landscape.

"Huh?"

"Ask," she said flatly, shifting in her seat. "It's ironic that you are concerned with crossing boundaries with art, yet not with other people's sex lives."

"As far as I could tell," I said, confused, "you seemed pretty receptive."

"Once we got into it," she said. "If you only would have asked, we could have cleared some things up first, made sure of a few things, so that today wouldn't have to be so uncomfortable."

I suddenly recalled the shot I had taken of the man emerging from the subway in Paris. Instantly, he had brought his hand up to cover his face from the view of my camera. Despite his obvious disapproval, I had gone ahead and taken the shot anyway, hand over his face and all. It made me sick now to think of it: invading his privacy as I had.

Why had I done this to him? Was this characteristic of me? Where was my pride?

My kindergarten class picture came to mind in a flash. All the children had smiled for the camera except me—I had covered my face with my hands. I had tried so hard to hide that I'd ended up making myself a freak. People later looked at the photo and the first place their eyes would go was to me, the awkward girl with her hands covering her face.

Perhaps I hadn't evolved at all, but just switched positions, from nervous subject to photographer.

Tears welled up and I covered my eyes. A gentle hand touched my back. It was, of course, Natasha's.

"I don't think you should take this too hard," she began. "I just wanted to bring it to your attention." She rubbed her palm back and forth across my hand, as though I were a child and she was a comforting parent. "Your contradiction."

The frumpy woman seated across from us stopped snoring, opened her eyes and looked at me. I wondered for a moment how much of our conversation she had listened to, but then decided not to care, wiping my tears away.

"What about *your* contradiction?"

Natasha looked at me as though she didn't know what I was referring to, her eyebrows raised high again.

"You force me to take shots of you and an old man in a Speedo at a beach and then you claim to respect people's privacy," I explained. "You look down on me for playing things safe while you eat at places like Hard Rock Café and later scold me for trying to be daring. It's as though you can do no wrong. What books have you read? I want them," I said, my voice trembling. "And you act like you are enjoying yourself, only for me later to find out that you aren't. 'I can't wait to get to Italy. I can't wait to get to Paris. Oh, I hate Italy. And fuck Paris. Oh, and fuck you, too, Danielle.' The fact is, you hate everything, Natasha. And it seems like everything you hate is always justified by theories, and you have a theory for everything because you fuck up everything!"

"I wish I had a mirror for you right now. Listen to yourself. Your anger towards me isn't necessary. You're throwing this all in my face." Her voice was calm again, as easy as that. I was no longer worth her stress. "I think we just want different things. It was just one night, Danielle," she said casually and turned back to face the window. "Let it go."

My head ached now. The older woman across from us looked down at her feet, rubbed them together and smiled.

"You young ladies like tarot card reading? I have a deck of cards in my bag. You have one together. I split price."

Neither of us answered.

The woman made a sour face and crossed her arms, then went for her cards, pulling them out of a small pouch and shuffling them quickly and precisely, as only years of practice can manage.

"How much?" Natasha asked.

The woman placed the stack of cards on the seat booth next to her. "For you, thirty."

"Thirty?"

"I'm the best," the woman said, licking a finger and spreading the deck out like a fan.

"Too much," Natasha said.

The woman tapped her finger against her head. "But I know the stars."

I looked at Natasha. "That's only ten American dollars."

"I don't have a wealthy family to support me," she snapped. Her eyes quickly became like needles. "Do you know that when my mother dropped me off at the airport, she asked if she could borrow sixty-five dollars for a phone bill?"

"You should have said no," I said.

"Oh, and like you can say no to your mother? You just avoid her, that's all. Except when you want money."

I turned towards the window, trying to keep my tears from resurfacing. I took a deep breath and exhaled long and slow.

"If I had your money," Natasha said, "I could really be someone."

In a flurry, I opened up my wallet, grabbed all the travelers' checks from inside—a few hundred dollars worth—and threw them onto the seat next to Natasha. "Here! Here, take it. It's all yours. I don't need it. It won't make me happy. Here, here. Go get famous or whatever. *Be* someone!"

Natasha started laughing a low, guttural laugh. She didn't touch the money.

"You're going to buy my love now?"

I looked across at the old woman, slowly cutting her deck and watching us like an insect, barely moving, trying not to call attention to herself, as though she could camouflage her presence with stillness.

I leaned over and picked the checks up off the booth seat. Natasha didn't move, silently watching me.

She knew all my contradictions now—my fears and flaws fully exposed. From the start of this trip, I'd been standing in bad lighting.

"And by the way," she said. "I'm not the fucker."

Later, on the train, I started my period. It was heavy and thick and painful, such pain that made me want to curl up in a ball and shake until all the pain would seep back into my bones. I also had a bit of trouble in the bathroom because of the water I'd drunk. The train rattled and shook as I tried to relieve myself, the inside cabin lights flickering on and off like an old film strip. I felt so dehydrated I was nearly delirious.

Back in my seat, I fell asleep again and dreamed of a gaunt girl with red hair who took a needle to her arm, a syringe filled with red liquid. I asked her what it was and she brought the needle to my mouth and dropped a little onto my tongue, eyes seducing me. It tasted sharp and salty.

Fuck drugs, she said, squeezing out a few drops more. I want your blood.

Hours later, when everyone else was asleep, I threw my tampon out the window of our coach car, too lazy to trek back to the bathroom.

Breasts aching, I stepped off the exit ramp, feeling as though my luggage had doubled in weight. I felt like a pack-horse, wishing I'd traveled lighter. Two young lovers kissed before departing, saying their good-byes. They had the same dyed black hair and were sharing headphones—one on each of their ears, perhaps wanting to score their good-bye with a shared song.

My insides stirred as though my muscles were wrestling in gravel. My heart cramped. Something within wanted to let go of things, to flood over the edge and out of sight, sinking away like the city behind us, never to be seen again.

Chapter 8

Ringing the Walls

Charles University. Arrival at last. Stopping inside a rest room to splash my face with cool water. Standing inside the university courtyard, acquainting myself with Dr. Friedlander and classmates. Relishing fresh air. White chairs lined up across the grass. Tables spread with cheeses and drinks. Natasha was already into the wine, obviously unhappy to be there, avoiding others while I took refuge in the new company and a lemon Fresca.

Some of our classmates were American, some not. This was evident by their clothing. So far, Prague women seemed to dress in an androgynous style that Americans steered away from—dark pants and sweaters blending into one another. Something about their faces seemed ambiguous, too. Even serious. Dr. Friedlander was talking to some of these local students, pointing out different areas of the campus, arms crossed over his chest. It occurred to me that he must enjoy his job.

I noticed an African-American woman with large, wide eyes and long spiral-curled hair.

As if on cue, she came over and introduced herself.

"I'm Valerie," she said, and hugged me—perhaps her version of a handshake. Her hair smelled like cigarette smoke.

"So you're the mysterious Valerie."

"How was the trip?" Valerie asked. "Make any connections?"

I contemplated asking Valerie why she never showed for coffee, but decided against it.

"Yeah, I think so . . . some," I said, not ready to spill my guts about art or love with a total stranger.

I could sense Natasha's ears in our conversation, as mine leaned her way. She was speaking to someone about the Louvre with what I thought was a forced enthusiasm: "Yes, I'd wanted to go to Paris for so long. Now I can say that I've seen the *Mona Lisa*."

"I hear you're weird." Valerie grinned slyly.

I forgot, for a moment, to breathe, and my face flushed with heat.

"How could anyone in Prague know anything about me?" I asked, noticing how defensive I must have sounded.

Valerie shrugged her shoulders and repeated herself, matter-of-factly, "I hear you're weird, that's all."

I absently checked the lens cap on my camera and Valerie started to laugh. "Say, don't you think you've checked that thing enough? You've already checked it twice since we've been talking. What would Freud say?"

She was right. It was becoming my nervous habit, and she'd been the only one to call it to my attention. "I don't know," I said. "I'll have to think about that."

"I don't think you'd want to know." She giggled.

Dr. Friedlander introduced the group. Half were locals, one woman was from Japan and the rest of us were from UCLA.

We were shown to our quarters and I was glad to finally

rest. It turned out that due to a cancellation by another student, Valerie never joined us as a third roommate and sleeping arrangements had shifted so that Natasha and I were left sharing a double. It relieved me since our initial meeting left me so confused. I still couldn't guess why Valerie had said what she had. If she was referring to my affair with Natasha, it bewildered me to think how anyone else could have known about it when we'd only just arrived in Prague. I wondered if Natasha was a gossip.

Our room was designed in the style of a dorm room with two small beds, two desks, two lamps, and two closets. My belly was cramping even more than it had earlier. I swallowed two aspirin and sat on the edge of my bed with a bottle of water. Natasha unzipped her suitcase and everything spilled out onto the floor.

"Made any connections?" she said, mimicking Valerie's question, obviously testing me.

"What you and I did together is private," I said.

"Are you ashamed?" she asked, without looking at me.

Natasha could shed her youthful affectations quickly when angered. Bitterness added ten years to her face. Her temper seemed impossible to face, if not, follow. Again, I had offended her, or annoyed her, and I couldn't begin to understand why.

"I'm not ashamed," I shot back.

"Did you notice how Dr. Friedlander didn't invite one boy on this trip?"

"I hadn't," I said. "But the students are all quite attractive, especially Valerie."

Natasha twisted her mouth into a supercilious grin, grabbed her cigarettes, and left the room.

★ ★ ★

In class, Dr. Friedlander lectured on the history of Czech poetry, and then, for the Czech students, he covered some of our great American poets.

"Something we all have in common," he said, his eyes meeting each student's eyes, one by one, "is passion. What does it mean, anyway, to feel passion? And secondly, how do we express it to another person?" He ran his hands through his hair and paced over to his desk, where he picked up his coffee mug and raised it, as if toasting. "That was the quest of our Romantic poets."

Friedlander set a daily itinerary:

11:00A.M.: begin day writing alone in cafés
3:00P.M.: meet at campus for a lecture and to share work (if willing)
7:00P.M.: begin evening with a group absinthe toast
8:00P.M.: excursion into Old Town

I found my morning fix at a tea shop on the edge of Prague. As recommended, I'd take my shoes off at the door, and follow the narrow oriental carpet runner into a dark parlor, my bare feet cooling against the slabs of concrete that separated each rug. I sat on a small beaded cushion and waited for something sweet and hot to arrive. When my drink of choice would finally come, I would hold the cup under my nose and breathe deeply. It was tea made from a red bush extract and I was soon addicted. It tasted sharp, rusty, and gritty, but seemed to be just what my taste buds wanted.

And so the day's routine would begin.

My life now appeared careless, next to other artists. Back home at school, I hadn't been exposed to the daily lives of my peers. Our relationships existed solely in the classroom, promptly ending when the hour had closed and I would anxiously depart. That had been my rhythm. Now I couldn't escape, and had to succumb to engaging in group activities. But escape from my camera and my thoughts was my new refuge, and I welcomed it without question.

As a class we toured the Gothic and Baroque churches: St. Nicholas, the Church of Our Lady, the Cathedral of St. Vitas. We viewed "the hanging hand," perhaps Prague's *Mona Lisa* of sights: a rotting gray limb dangled from the ceiling of the cathedral, desiccated fingers still attached. Stained-glass windows fully illuminated its every hideous and knotty detail.

There was the Abbey of the Slaves, the National Theater and Museum Building, built during the fourteenth century, and Kafka's house, where he had spent his formative years. I was especially taken with the Old Town Hall's astronomical clock, which kept several kinds of time including "Bohemian time," and the Charles Bridge—all built with a spirit of beautiful simplicity. I didn't photograph them, however, or even strive to write about them in my journal, or try them out as subjects for poems. My opinion seemed of no value anymore.

Nights consisted of dinner, opera, and nightcaps lasting until early morning, all which could be had for just a few dollars.

I was along only for the ride, and I relinquished all effort. I even contemplated the idea of returning home and ending my travels early, but decided to stick it out, if only for Mother's sake.

Let her get her money's worth.

Natasha wandered off to Prague Castle to write, possibly still searching for her knight in shining armor. She often read aloud in class from her works in progress, and began many of her poems with excerpts from Grimm's fairy tales, mixing metaphors, using terms like "snow" and "icing" in reference to drug use. She read them to the class in a trembling voice.

"I don't understand," a Prague student shared after one of Natasha's readings. "The poem seems very childish." Her words had taken on a harsher tone than intended, due to the language barrier. Natasha fled from the room, looking as if she were about to cry. Her platform sandals clicked loudly against the hallway until we couldn't hear them anymore.

Friedlander demanded we let her be, telling us that artists are sensitive creatures and yet, they need to learn to accept criticism. "That is, if you are to become the greatest writers of your generation. All artists need to acquire this stamina."

Whenever my time came to offer a reading, I passed. I had written nothing so far. Restless hours were spent in cafés— aimless words mumbled into teacups, never finding their way to the page. All I seemed to do was recall the conversations I'd had earlier on the trip with Natasha, wondering where and how I'd gone wrong.

After a couple weeks had passed, I learned something new: that Natasha had an obsession with color and perfumes, especially flowers. I began to see how even with very little money, she could find meaning, beauty, and serenity. I would catch her from afar, smelling roses in a public garden with an almost perverse determination, her nose buried in the center, petals spread about her cheeks. Despite the fact that people smelled flowers all the time, I somehow sexualized the otherwise innocent actions on Natasha's part of walking up to a flower and plunging her nose into its central, most sensitive reproductive place to inhale, with its heart of pistils, so clitoral-

like and its labia-like stamens that softly blanketed the surrounding area. I was, perhaps, even jealous and began to stalk
her, to some extent, having nothing else to do.

I watched her wander into the Museum Legenda Argondie,
located just west of the Charles Bridge. It was a local gallery,
which I quietly explored as I trailed behind her. The gallery
was owned by a Czech surrealist painter named Reon, whose
own image resembled that of his paintings and his gallery—
idealized, elfin, and slightly distorted. He looked like an old
king: bearded, overdressed, with long hair tied in the center of
his back, carrying an elaborately carved cane with a glass ball
at its top. Tables and throne-like chairs were offered to tourists
to sit and contemplate the portfolios of Reon's work, to perhaps seduce them into purchases. There were carafes of red
wine and deep half-filled goblets littered about a center table,
inviting the tourists to relax, let loose, and wander into his
surreal world. The building resembled a magical, allegorical
cave: the walls drooped low, its interior was filled with sculptures,
fountains, and mystical airbrushed paintings of doe-eyed
princesses and mermaids with blue-green eyes and purple fins,
dreamily gazing at their own noses. Cross-eyed! Yes. Something
about these paintings of nymphs was adolescent. Vulgar! The
way Reon drew the breasts—overly high-set, as though he'd
never seen or caressed a real pair. Nevertheless, Natasha fell in
love with Reon's work, trying to express her gratitude and
admiration to the artist in her broken French. *"Je t'aime,"* she
kept repeating. *"Je t'aime."* And she was not alone. Many other
tourists held the gallery Argondie in high acclaim, purchasing
expensive prints and loitering in his gallery with joints and
wine bottles, their eyes pink and glazed over, their faces dumb
and jolly. It made me question the connection between drug
use and idealism, since so many of Reon's patrons seemed to
have an appreciation for getting stoned.

I watched all of this from afar, a voyeur. The distance enabled me to objectively analyze her—to try to make sense of the chasm that had opened between us.

Inside our room, I began observing Natasha as though she were a stranger. I watched her write late into the night. She wrote all her poetry with pen and ink, the old way, having purchased her stationery in exotic paper shops. She'd let her hair grow in beneath her arms and on her legs, perhaps trying to be less American, or perhaps in an effort to just let go.

I recalled the satisfied smile on Natasha's face the last time she had read her work in class. She'd apparently recovered from the trauma of the initial insult, or perhaps, decided to mask her reactions to class criticism. A couple of times, she had looked up at Valerie for her response. They had been exchanging looks lately.

Late one night, lying in bed with my eyes closed, I heard Natasha whisper, "She was my lover. Valerie. She was my ex. I haven't been with a man for a long time." Her voice sounded disturbed and foreign, not her own. Perhaps she was talking in her sleep. I didn't ask. I just lay there, stiff, hoping I would appear asleep.

It now made sense: Valerie's disinterest in meeting us for coffee that first time, Natasha's constant scrutiny of Valerie's behavior. I wondered what had originally brought them together, as well as what had driven them apart.

It made me feel sick to think that Natasha had had any reason to lie, that she was carrying around photos of a man no longer in her life, and whom she might not have been as close to as I'd thought.

Natasha was more scared than I was.

★ ★ ★

Night after night, and every morning, I watched her. I watched her sleep, and wake. Lying so still. Shallow breaths. Clutching her pillow she'd brought from home.

I wanted her again. I wanted to be brave with her. To never leave the room we shared. But there seemed no sense in trying to reach her now. She was writing constantly, and I wondered if this isolation was part of her process.

Late one morning, in a silent place such as this, filled with only questions and no answers, I began to masturbate, quietly at first so that Natasha wouldn't know. My hand beneath the covers, careful not to stir too much or move too fast. Careful not to breathe too heavily. But then I decided—all too aware of her presence in the room—that she was the reason for my hunger and that there was no sense in hiding anymore.

"I want to touch myself," I said abruptly, no seduction intended. "Will this make you uncomfortable?"

There was a pause. I could tell she was nervous. "Uh, no," she said plainly. "That's cool."

I didn't hold back anymore, in movement or breath. I kept the sheet across my body, but claimed my space, the rights I had to my sexuality and my pleasure. In doing so, I became aware, even more so, of her presence in the room. She was right there with me. Listening. I could hear her soft breaths.

Afterwards, I slid my jeans on and went outside. The cool air felt refreshing against my warm cheeks and neck. I walked through town and rented a bicycle near the Charles Bridge, then pedaled over to the castle where Natasha had been spending her days. She'd been writing about the castle in her poetry she read in class, and I wanted to see it for myself, this place that set her mind into dreams.

At the castle grounds, I parked my bicycle and walked the perimeter twice, getting a thorough look. A woman wearing a wide-brimmed hat was leaving the grounds, strolling alone, holding the long slit of her skirt together so as not to over-expose her bare leg.

The castle was smaller than I had imagined, but when I thought of Natasha there, smiling, writing in her Asian floral journal, I began to appreciate its subtleties.

I lay on the expansive lawn in front of the fort, beneath a large tree, and closed my eyes. Somewhere, off in the hills, a group of musicians drummed and played pan flutes. With my belly pressed to the earth, I dug my toes into the cool grass.

I recalled a time from my past. The memory surprised me, the incident having happened when I was about ten. My mother had been braiding my hair when she'd caught sight of some hair beneath my armpit, then asked if she could look at it again. I didn't want to show it to her, as it seemed no one's business but my own. She'd said, "That probably means you have hair someplace else, too, doesn't it?" Blood had rushed to my face and I had burned with embarrassment. It was self-ish of Mother. She had no respect for my privacy.

I opened my eyes. In front of me were long blades of grass, whispering to me, it seemed.

The day my mother had discovered my puberty was one of the times I recalled a great chasm opening between what I felt was my own and what I felt might partially belong to others. In many ways, I was still in the same place, standing next to my mother's bed as she combed with short, sharp strokes, electrifying my hair with static.

A bulldozer began to work somewhere nearby, digging

and backing up and dumping, a caution-tone repeating almost continuously. I closed my eyes and lay my head back down against the grass. It smelled like children's hair.

"Have you ever had a ménage à trois?" Natasha asked, a few nights later. She had come in from a bar, somewhat earlier than usual. I was lounging across my single bed, flipping through a local theater guide, looking at the film stills. She hadn't said hello, or asked how I was, but had plopped down on the edge of my bed with a confidence prompted by alcohol.

"Yes."

"Really?" she asked, showing more curiosity about me than she had for weeks. She stretched herself out on my mattress and propped her chin on her hands. "Tell me everything."

I did not like the way in which she so suddenly resumed our intimacy after such a long period of estrangement.

"That information is private."

"Aren't we quite private?" She giggled.

The smell of malt liquor emerged from her mouth, raunchy yet sensual. I wondered what had stimulated her to ask the question and where she intended it to lead.

"It depends on how you look at things," I hedged.

"Yes, everything does, doesn't it?" She smiled.

She was annoying me. Despite wanting to be close to her, I actually wished that I had my evening to myself tonight. Her mysteriousness was painful for me.

"Listen," I said, closing the magazine. "Did you come back only to harass me?"

She gave me a look. "Why would I do that?"

Then she began to undress. Off went her top, then her jeans. She was left in her bra and panties, another lacy set that made me want her again.

I didn't feel like answering her question. "You really want to know about my ménage à trois?"

"I don't know," she said, turning onto her back and looking up at the ceiling. Her stomach appeared extremely flat with her in that position. "I think I'd rather just experience it." She rolled quickly back so that she was facing me. She looked longingly at me, raising an eyebrow in her customary way, her cleavage shadowy and deep. "With you."

I swallowed, scared that she was heading down a path that could involve even more heartbreak for me. "Why?"

She turned on her back again, looking dreamily up at the ceiling, searching for words. There was silence, as she started then stopped several times to answer me. Finally she just shrugged and unhooked the front of her bra, her gorgeous breasts falling from their harness. She let the lace bra drop to the floor. "Why not?"

I was confused. She'd spoken of a ménage a trois, but it was only the two of us in the room, and her clothes were already off, ready for bed.

Waking up next to her again, bodies exposed and touching, her warm breath rising and falling next to mine, was a fantasy I'd given up on. Now, the possibility of it happening made me fear another lengthy period of punishment such as had happened after that gloomy day in Paris.

I still considered the risk one worth taking, whatever happened as a result.

And then she crashed.

★　★　★

Spread out next to me on my bed, snoring, Natasha had managed to make me feel the fool again. When she woke up sober, would she even remember her proposition? She breathed in and out evenly. Her breath was almost fierce, suggesting the lingering effects of hard alcohol. Like a man's liquor breath. I found a credit card receipt on the bed, next to her. It was from the Cavern pub and she had charged several pints of beer and a few harder drinks as well.

I took another look at Natasha's naked skin. Tempted as I was to touch and kiss her, to try to do this so as to only please her and not to disrupt her sleep, I thought of an entirely different option, one which I had not allowed myself to consider:

I could abandon her.

I now knew what kind of investment I had in this woman: none. Because she obviously had none in me. No longer getting any real return from her company, I thought of the saying I always came back to, about the definition of insanity, and decided that I no longer wanted to keep walking on eggshells to try to please her.

I was ready to abandon the scene. And so I did, slipping into a skirt I had not yet worn, brushing my hair out, putting on makeup, and locking the door behind me. I was bent upon a night out, determined to have a good time without Natasha.

At the Bottle Party Cavern, a locals' bar lit with flaming torches at the entrance, I spotted Valerie quietly sipping a tall stein of beer. I asked if I could join her.

She nodded at the empty seat next to her. "Sit down, weirdo," she said warmly.

As I sat down, Valerie gave me a skeptical grin.

"So, Danielle, what's the story with you and Natasha?" Her voice was a little slurred from the alcohol she'd been drinking. "I've seen the way you look at her." Valerie took another sip of her drink. Her comment left me feeling more exposed than I would have liked. I raised my hand, signaling the bartender for a beer.

There were candles with red glass hurricane lamps placed over them on every table, giving the room a rosy, muted glow. I was grateful for the dim lighting.

"I feel different about her than I have toward other women."

"This the first time you've fallen in love with a woman?" Valerie burst out laughing, beer spilling from her lips and from the glass she held. "I'm sorry to laugh," she said, covering her mouth. "It's just—you look so serious."

"What makes you think I've fallen in love?" I asked.

"Natasha told me. She said you need a mother."

Her frankness shocked me into silence. Perhaps it was the quality Natasha had found attractive in her. But what she said struck a chord in me, although I immediately took issue with the observation.

"I've already got a mother, one who reminds me daily how I'm wasting her money with this art degree and that only fools try to make their hobbies into careers. She thinks art is for children and the retired. I'm beginning to wonder, actually, if she might not be right."

The bartender handed me my beer and I took a large gulp.

"Holy shit! Look who needs rescuing."

The comment made me feel sick. I didn't want to be sitting there anymore. Because it was true. I did want to be rescued. I wanted to be picked up by a great bird on his huge, enveloping wings, which would carry me from everyone and everything that made me feel like a failure.

"If only I could start over," I said, swallowing.

"Uh-huh. Start over where?"

"At the beginning," I said, without hesitation. I took another swallow from my glass.

Valerie turned to me, pulling her hair away from her face so I could see her eyes. "You've come a long way from when I saw you on campus. You were so reserved back then."

"So you've seen me around?"

"Yeah, I've seen you. I notice all the girls. Hasn't Natasha told you about that habit of mine?"

I shook my head.

"It's a habit of Natasha's, too."

"Are you still in love with her?" I asked.

"Girl, you are a fool!" Valerie laughed, wrinkling her nose. "Of course I am. Who isn't?" Then she sighed. "I'm jealous of you, Danielle. You've got Natasha's attention. But when it comes right down to it, you'll be alone again, too, like all of us. Nothing lasts."

Valerie's eyes had been darting across the bar to a man who I'd noticed eyeing Valerie from the time I'd walked in. She apparently was aware he'd been watching her. He was dark-eyed and had a cleft chin.

"So you like men, too?" I observed. "Don't you have a preference?"

"I just enjoy the moments," she said, getting up. "As you should." Without saying good-bye, she walked toward the man, leaving me alone at the bar. Glancing back at me, she laughed.

"Freedom can be a beast," she said, as she put her arm around the man's thick neck and pulled him to her, as if to devour him. However, he surprised me by turning to me, motioning with his hand for me to join them. Only later did it occur to me that I was living out a scene that night that Natasha had most probably intended to enact herself.

The flat was on the river and was owned by the man, Xavier. He was bearded and quiet and I could not tell his age, but his body beneath his clothes was strong and lean and I had a feeling that I was in for some pleasant surprises.

Xavier lit a fire in a living room which faced the river and instantly the room grew warm. We all took off our sweaters and sat in our T-shirts near the fireplace, sipping the small glasses of brandy he had poured us. The brandy was thick and brown and tasted like syrup to me. It warmed my body all the way into my belly.

In the glow of the fire, Valerie appeared different than she had before, taller and more aggressive, her beauty somehow intimidating. She leaned toward the flames, looking back over her shoulder at me from time to time, smiling enigmatically. I was becoming frightened of what was to come.

"You're nervous," Xavier observed. "You can't have fun when you're nervous."

Valerie let out a low giggle. "Oh, yes you can."

Upon hearing this, I stiffened.

"Let's frighten her," Valerie said, looking over at me. "I think she'd like it."

"I think *you'd* like it," Xavier said to Valerie.

The moments that followed happened so quickly, I can barely recall them. The two of them stripped me and lifted me onto the only significant piece of furniture in the room, a table. I was laid across it, with my arms and legs tied to its legs. I neither consented nor protested. Naked and splayed out, I felt longer and bonier than ever, but my seducers seemed to like what they saw, so I tried to relax into the moment.

I had to admit that I wanted this to happen.

Valerie pulled up her sleeves and directed Xavier to sit in one of the chairs, to just watch.

Within the course of the next hour I was put through a series of small tortures, as she would repeatedly bring me close to orgasm and then pull me back, leaving me to yearn and even beg for release. I wasn't really attracted to Valerie, but I was turned on by the power over me that I had given her. For those hours, I had put them in charge of disbursing pleasure to me, and I had chosen to be obedient.

As Valerie was licking me below, I came out of my dreamy state long enough to wonder how Natasha would react to what was going on, whether she would be angry or, perhaps, jealous. Then the erotic sensations engulfing all my nerves took over and extinguished Natasha from my mind entirely. But just before I was about to give in to the waves of sensation that were being created between my legs by Valerie's exquisite tongue manipulations, she pulled back and smiled at me. I wished I'd pretended not to have been as excited as I was so she would have taken me through to my climax. Instead she said, "Now it's time for me to watch."

Valerie released me from the table, untying my arms and legs. They felt stiff and a little sore since they'd been moving to and fro so much against their restraints, as I'd strained to wrap myself more tightly around the source of my pleasure while I was being licked and caressed. Now, more than anything, I wanted to lunge toward Valerie and let her take me the rest of the way, but Xavier was already making his way toward me.

I sat on the floor, the throbbing wetness between my legs almost unbearable. It was as though I was in a theater, and had just stepped offstage, mid-scene.

Valerie now sat in Xavier's abandoned chair and held a

dildo in her hands. She ran her fingers firmly along the length of it.

Xavier kneeled down and placed two fingers inside of me. I could smell my own sex and even hear my moistness as he caressed me. Sighs of pleasure escaped me as he inserted his fingers part way in, and then, just as I opened farther, inviting him in deeper, he would pull his fingers out, causing me to moan at his withdrawal.

"This is Xavier's specialty," Valerie suddenly said. "Teasing."

Valerie pulled down her pants enough to insert the silicone dildo into herself, her ankles lifted above her seat. The wood of her chair cracked as she let out a gasp and began to emulate with the dildo what Xavier was doing to me with his fingers. From where Xavier and I were, we could see everything.

"I want to fuck," I whispered to Xavier.

Without a word he slid a condom onto himself so quickly and smoothly that I hardly knew what was happening. Then I was ordered to get onto my knees.

He came at me from the back, my legs slightly spread as his lubricated penis slipped inside of me, cool and very wet. The fit was effortless as I was so ready to receive him. He reached his hand around my front as he penetrated me, tickling my clitoris with the tips of his fingers until I began to quiver. Slightly self-conscious, I glanced over to see Valerie now working the dildo into herself with a skill that seemed very practiced. Her face was contorted into an expression that seemed near tears, and then she began to wail a cry of ecstasy.

Just before I came, Xavier withdrew himself from me and inserted his lovely wet tongue again. I instantly rolled onto my back and wrapped my legs around his head, wanting to finally have my way. I came for a prolonged time, convulsing again and again against his face. His cheeks felt as soft and damp as the petals of a rose.

I gave into an affair with my camera and began shooting photographs again. I consciously avoided the static still lifes I had captured before. Art was all around me, I realized, and I only had to look to find it. Truth was there, waiting to tell me its secrets.

I went to a local camera shop and developed the rolls I'd taken thus far on our trip, so I could get the full range of what I'd done. I sat on a curb outside the lab and studied the proof sheets from Venice, the ones with the man in the Speedo. I'd taken a couple of shots, and actually preferred the one where Natasha had started to walk away, leaving the older man sadly looking down at himself, which said more about the moment than the forced smiles did. If sadness was this honest, then I preferred it.

There were the shots of Natasha on the gondola. I only began to understand them now, now that they were before me in full view. Her skin appeared almost translucent in the photos, the sunlight illuminating her so that the veins beneath the surface were revealed and vulnerable, blood pumping just below. Her nipples were a blazing red.

And the man in the Paris metro, exiting, his hand covering his face. Although I might have caught him off guard, it could have been disturbing for him to have been captured with a mass of people, exiting a densely packed subway, living a common life—an image he might not have wanted his face connected to. Or perhaps he was just caught somewhere that he shouldn't have been that morning. Either way, this image contained all his truth.

The photos hadn't been a mistake, but rather, the part of

myself I had come to like: for the first time, I was really seeing people.

Three weeks in Prague. I was having tea with Mee Jun,
my Asian classmate, after we'd attended a photography exhibit
together. The exhibit had been a showcase of Prague artists,
many of whose works depicted a realism I could not dream
of achieving. On a whim and feeling exceptionally brave, I
opened my backpack and shared my recent work with the
gallery owner.

The man spoke good English. "You have an interesting
eye," he said. "Have you considered doing a show of your
own?"

I explained to him that I felt that I didn't have enough
material for a show, but that I would let him know when I
did.

"Please do," he said, and handed me his card.

It was the greatest compliment I'd ever had for my work.

"I feel high, like I can do anything," I said to Mee Jun,
sipping my tea in the teahouse.

"Your body is made new," she said, her translation a bit
jarring, and yet, interesting in its freshness.

We discussed her life and the older man who had funded
her studies abroad—studies otherwise unaffordable to her.
She was living with him and he wanted to marry her, but had
no idea she had an eleven-year-old daughter from a previous
relationship, who was now living with Mee Jun's mother. She
said the real reason she had kept this information from him
was because he didn't know she was in her early forties, and
thought her about twenty-eight years old and had been a virgin until they had met.

Mee Jun secretly took lovers, younger men in their mid-twenties with whom she was honest about her situation, her age, and her daughter. She said she prayed every day that one of these young men would marry her and that she could be reunited with her daughter.

"Won't it be hard to gain a man's trust if he knows you are lying to someone else already?" I asked.

"I have no alternative," she said. "Financial security is the most important thing and I must do it this way."

I asked if I could photograph her.

"Why me?" she asked, her expression both flattered and somewhat self-conscious. Her smile faded in and out.

"Because," I explained, looking at her and wondering if there was a way of capturing her mixture of both hope and doom, "you're human."

I paid our bill and we went over to the bridge where I had Mee Jun lean out and look down at the water. There were ducks below, which she pointed out, looking back at the camera, straight into the lens—an expression of desperate trust.

"You're very complex," I said, more prepared to say something about her mind than her physical beauty. She was undoubtedly pretty, with pearl-like skin and full lips, thick black hair twisted up into a loose bun. But her real beauty came from inside, an incurable faith that made me both excited and sad. Inside her lived desires she couldn't face—desires, no doubt, having to do with real fulfillment, independence, and love.

"I am so glad to know you," she said, suddenly laughing, breaking the seriousness of the moment. "I could kiss you."

About a week later, I asked a local Czech woman if she would like to pose for me in exchange for a meal at a proper restaurant in town. She was a large-bellied woman, thick-legged, with sensuous lips that begged one's attention, and she carried her body as though it were thin. She reminded me of a young woman with whom I'd gone to grade school. A girl who thought she was skinny, when in fact she was quite obese. She would dress in skimpy tops and skirts, daring her classmates to look at her and the skirt, which was rising high on her very full and creamy thighs. I'd developed a little crush on her, despite the fact that I believed myself quite heterosexual then, and on top of that, quite "picky." Perhaps it was this act of deception, in and of itself, that was the girl's charm?

We decided to shoot at her place and, without my even having to ask, the stranger stripped off all her clothing and I photographed her in her kitchen next to the sink, where she had been dying scarves earlier that day. I asked her to continue with her task, naked, while I shot her at work.

At first the whole thing was awkward, nonsensical, and posed, but towards the end as she was draping the scarves across her body so the dye could dry, the colors bled onto her skin, producing the most unusual shapes, like animal spots. And then I felt it—that feeling that I was getting closer to something which I had been long searching for. A feeling that was becoming familiar.

Rotten apple cores, yogurt tubs, and empty bottles littered Natasha's half of the room, although, as neat as I was, it didn't bother me. I saw less and less of her, and any signs from her secret life were welcomed. Often, she would not enter our dorm until early in the morning, waking me as her breath filled the room with the stench of beer. She purchased a pon-

cho and wore it almost constantly, as though she were hiding.
As far as I could tell, she hadn't met her destined knight.

She would silently enter class, now wearing flat sandals,
her eyes avoiding others and straying toward a window for
escape. Whenever possible, she avoided activities organized
outside of the class, or just followed behind the group in the
shadows, smoking her long cigarettes or scribbling frantically
in her journal. Students gossiped at first, then gradually forgot
about Natasha and paid her no attention. This surprised me,
how uncurious they all seemed, posing as "artists," there to
practice the art of poetry and poetic living within a group, yet
closed to the potency of its members.

The same went for Valerie, who proved true to her statement about living for the moments. She seemed to release
our night of pleasure as though it had been a simple party and
nothing else. Although it was hard for me to look at her in
the same way after all we'd been through, I accepted our
promiscuous night together as another unexpected detour in
my travels that summer, and learned to better accept the otherwise familiar undercurrents: an occasional tender smile, as
well as the dreamy, knowing stares. The more I thought about
it, the more I decided that Valerie and Natasha might have
made an excellent couple, so alike they were when it came to
fickleness.

As a class, we attended the opera houses. I acquired a
habit of wearing a scarf given to me by the woman I had
photographed. I'd begun to wear eye makeup as well, deciding that my eyes were my best asset and they should not be
hidden. I'd also gained some weight, courtesy of the local
food. I thought this extra weight flattered my figure.

Seated high in the immense theaters, surrounded by all
the acoustics, reinvigorated me with a sense of passion and

wonder for who I was becoming. I was listening to Mozart in Prague. I looked down at the great arena below, unfrightened of the height at which we were seated. I had the Eiffel Tower behind me. I could climb anything now.

Natasha appeared numb throughout the performances. We would all be crying, the music climaxing, and I'd glance over to Natasha and find her sitting as still as glass.

One night when we were in a restaurant as a group, Natasha picked a fight with Dr. Friedlander, who'd accused her of drinking "a lot."

"A bottle of wine is not *a lot*," she'd said.

He begged to differ.

"Four glasses," she said, slowly raising her fingers. "I should know. I pour the stuff in restaurants back home every day."

Sometimes, on the weekends, I would see her stepping off a bus or trolley in a complete daze, not recognizing me. One time I saw her talking outside the campus with Friedlander. She seemed to be crying.

I found wrappers and sacks from McDonald's in the wastebasket of our room, and maps scattered about, relics from her exploring.

I had no idea where she'd gone.

I thought about the changes she had made thus far on our time together, and was astonished: she'd amputated her social connections and had taken to being alone. It was as though our roles had reversed.

I finally phoned Mother again, from the American Café. There was a pay phone in the back. Somewhat mesmerized by the visuals of drunken college students downing shots of absinthe, I tried to focus on Mother's words, plugging my other ear with my finger so I could hear her better.

"I don't understand why you won't call. It's as though you want to make things difficult between us. Are you trying to hide something?"

"What could I be hiding? How's your back?"

The song "YMCA" came on and a guy and girl climbed on top of the bar and started dancing, miming the song as I'd seen done at the other American restaurants. One of the girls was wearing a short skirt and I could look right at her underwear. Black G-string. The girl was so drunk she kept miming the wrong letters at the wrong times, and I started to crack up.

"Are you drunk?" Mother asked.

It seemed so pathetic now, my need to abide by her rules at all times, continuing to "check in" when I was perfectly safe, too safe perhaps.

"Are you listening to me?" She seemed to hear the loud music pumping in the background. "Are you at some sort of a wild party or something? What kind of music is that they play over there?"

"It's American music, Mother. I'm at the American Bar."

She breathed out long, seemingly relieved. "I hope you make some nice friends over there instead of wasting your summer away with fleeting relationships. You know, you've always made things so hard for yourself, and life shouldn't be hard. Just follow the rules, Danielle. Spend time with people whose life will be a success, and yours will be a success." There was a long pause on her end of the line. "Danielle? Why are you so quiet? Are you there?"

"Yes, Mother. I was listening to you."

"Wow," she said, letting out a long sigh. "That's a change."

"*I've* changed."

"I don't know what you are talking about," she said, somewhat surprised. "One summer can't change a person."

I decided, then, that it would be the last time I called before returning home.

The drunken guy dancing on the bar had started whistling and when I looked up, he extended his arms and motioned for me to climb up and join him. Like the girl, I, too, was wearing a dress, a knee-length Audrey Hepburn-style basic that I'd picked up at a vintage boutique in town, wanting to expand my wardrobe. Now I shook my head. The thought of standing on a countertop in a dress was too much.

My hands clasped the sides of my skirt and I peered down at it, wondering if it could stay put.

"I promise I won't look," the guy hollered out over the music, covering his eyes.

One of the girls below handed me a shot of ouzo. I took another shot after that, followed by three more. I kept thinking about Mother's comments on my fleeting relationships, wondering if I would ever have a relationship that would last. I wondered if the brevity of my relationships was something I had chosen, in the same way that I had chosen my path as a photographer, and of loving a woman.

I danced the "YMCA," along with many other dances. Sometimes I made up my own moves, and sometimes the couple sandwiched me between them and ground against me, one on either side. The differences between their bodies impressed me—her softness and his firm tall body. The drunken girl eventually became even drunker, and ended up sitting below with her girlfriends, nearly passed out, while I continued to dance with the guy. He looked at me and smiled.

"I love American," he said in a thick Czech accent.

I nodded and left to find the bathroom. Once inside, I looked into the mirror above the sink and saw my face—modern and confident, despite my drunkenness. For the first time, what I saw didn't surprise me.

"Good times," I whispered to my reflection.

I turned on the water faucet and washed my hands, which were sticky with ouzo from the shot glasses, and slipped out of the American Bar, down some steps and into Old Town's premier Jazz club—Jazz Zelezna. I had heard about it, and couldn't pass it up tonight when I heard the sounds of a live saxophone creeping up out of the club and into the streets. I wanted something different than Americana tonight.

I entered the Gothic basement, which felt like a medieval cellar. There was a full bar, barrel vaulted ceilings, air-conditioning. Bright lights flashed above a large wooden stage, where a three-piece band was playing, a saxophonist taking the lead. The saxophonist had a stocky build, and dark rings around his eyes, either from years of smoking or from lack of sleep. He was wearing a Bohemian crocheted hat and black wool vest, and he played a type of free-form jazz, defying the constraints that the other instruments seemed to follow—steady drum beats and rhythmic piano chords. Honking sounds came forth as he blew through his mouthpiece, his fingers running up and down the shaft of his horn, his eyes down. When he finally looked up, his eyes met mine and I looked away, suddenly shy. I found my way to a bar stool and ordered a beer.

The song had an eerie finish and the saxophone player let go of his instrument after one final blow, allowing the weight of the instrument to fall against his neck strap. He jumped off the stage and came over to the bar and ordered himself a beer. His voice was deep and coarse.

"This one's on me," I said, placing some money on the counter. "You are really good."

I noticed my words slurring a little as I said this.

"Thank you," he said, in a perfect American accent. "You're from the States?"

"L.A.," I said.

"I'm sorry to hear that," he said, with total seriousness, as he took his pint.

I offered him the empty stool next to me, but he shook his head. "Thanks, but I'm too wound up to sit just yet."

I took a closer look at him and noticed the bright color in his cheeks, and up close, the bags beneath his eyes—so dark and puffy. I imagined him staying up late into the nights, practicing his songs.

"My name's Jeremy," he said. He had a professional air about him.

"Danielle," I said, shaking the hand he offered. His skin felt hot.

"My sister's name is Danielle."

The bar was crowded and people were still coming in. A middle-aged couple entered and the woman sat on the empty seat next to me. I decided to donate my stool to the man and stood next to Jeremy while we drank our beers.

Recorded jazz came on over the house speakers, and the volume of the noisy crowd began to rise. I had to stand closer to Jeremy in order to hear him speak.

"I'm from Chicago, but I've been living in Prague the last nine months. They've actually got a pretty good jazz scene going, and it's easy for Americans to get along here," he said, reaching inside his vest and tugging on a pair of suspenders. "Dollars go a long way and there're lots of English-speaking

people—not that I need to talk. In this city, music is the language."

"But why not make music in America?"

"Good question." He took a large gulp from his pint.
"Too distracting. Too much of everyone trying to fit in and
acquire things—house, car, wife, pop-star image." He laughed.
"I started wanting all those things, too."

"What's wrong with wanting those things? Are they
bad?"

"For an artist, yes. Yes, if the intention is to merely have
what other people have. That fucks with the creative mind.
For an artist or a musician to say something from here," he
said, tapping his chest with the edge of his pint, "he or she
must think as a creator, not as an imitator. We have to follow
our own unique paths." His body was broad and firm, and my
eyes kept returning to that spot—his sternum—where he'd
pressed his beer glass.

"And what has Prague given you in return for your originality?" I asked.

He took a deep breath and gave me an ironic look, his
brows furrowed. "No house. No car. No real job. No wife."

I laughed. The lights on stage went blue and the canned
music faded out. I wondered if it was time for Jeremy to return to the stage.

I finished the last of my beer, then reached down and
grabbed my backpack off the floor, preparing to leave. "It was
nice meeting you, Jeremy. I'll come see you again."

"Want some company on your walk back?"

"Well," I said, looking around at the crowd of people.
"Don't you have to play?"

"I don't *have* to do anything," he said. "That's why I'm in
Prague, remember?"

The look on his face said he wasn't joking.

★ ★ ★

On the way back to my dorm, Jeremy led me on a series of detours through his favorite squares. We sat on the benches, pausing to rest, as I was winded from the alcohol I'd drunk.

"How did you learn to play the way you do?" I asked, aware that he hadn't used any sheet music when playing and had probably been improvising.

"I'm basically self-taught, but I've been tutored by some outstanding mentors here and there. They've encouraged and supported me to find my own voice, which is the greatest gift."

"Sounds Zen," I said.

"In many ways, free jazz and avant-garde jazz have a lot of parallels to Eastern philosophies. They came out of the sixties, and their aim was to destroy popular conventions and simply *let go* of all resistance. Some old-school jazz snobs hear me play and claim I lack technique, but what I'm doing is exciting—to me, at least. People don't realize that it takes a concentrated effort, not laziness, just to defy the constraints of orthodox harmony."

I liked what he was saying, and also the sound of his voice. I could have listened to him for hours. I felt so relaxed, almost ready for sleep.

"Why don't I play for you," he said, motioning toward the black case he had resting at his feet.

"Won't you wake the neighbors?" I whispered.

Jeremy looked around the courtyard. We were in a district of merchants with overhead apartments, quiet above the streets. To the other side of us was the river Vlatava.

"Passion sometimes wakes the neighbors." He shrugged, pulling out his shiny silver sax. He began playing chords in a serpentine style, then began to explore a more brooding melody, his horn yelping every now and then, as if to say, "don't fall asleep now."

My eyelids grew heavy and my calves were cold. I wasn't wearing any socks, I wasn't used to the sensation of fresh air blowing on my bare legs.

"Play something sentimental," I urged, leaning back on the bench.

Jeremy looked at me, licking his lips and putting his mouthpiece to the side for a moment. His dark eyes softened, and he seemed happy. "You want a ballad?"

"Something dead to ring the walls."

He made a quick nod, as though he understood, and brought the mouthpiece to his lips. As he did this, I felt myself moisten. I uncrossed my legs and stretched them out over Jeremy's lap.

It was a gloomy melody that snaked inside me—no strange goose honks or growls breaking the smoothness this time. His emotions seemed to be bubbling under the surface, not so obvious now, and it made both him and his music glow.

While playing, Jeremy was able to keep a melody, his thumb and pinky pressing the pads while the belled body of the instrument lay in his lap as his other hand slowly climbed my bare legs.

The evening air was vibrating from his melody, and I wondered why the whole city didn't come out running to better hear his beautiful song. Never before had I enjoyed music so much. I felt I was understanding it in a way that I hadn't before. It was as if we were having a conversation, except that we weren't even talking.

My blue paisley skirt had buttons all up the front. Slowly, Jeremy unbuttoned them with his free hand. He played, kissed my nipples, then went back to the mouthpiece, back and forth, from saxophone to my body, almost a ménage a trois. His lips were thick; his hair, a coal black storm of waves, which dangled below his ears and brushed against my neck when he kissed me. Its coarse texture made me relax into him. He was breathing hard. "Jazz is very effective this way." He made the horn produce a purring sound, then set it down.

I kicked off my sandals and he pressed his body against mine on the bench. In my intoxication I began to hallucinate a little. He pulled my skirt up and moved his fingers inside of me in a soft probing way. The fingers became an entity of their own, disconnected from him, and I forgot that he was there, or that I was there, outside in a courtyard—my body and insides fully exposed.

"I want . . . to love you," he said, peering into my eyes, looking at me as though he saw something deeper that I didn't know about. His brows were heavy and he grimaced and immediately drew back in embarrassment. "Oh, God, what am I saying?"

"You're just . . ." I began, wanting to tell him not to worry, that I understood it was just the moment, but he stopped me.

"I know what you're thinking," he whispered, placing his weathered hands under my chin, gently caressing the skin on my neck. "But that still doesn't explain this."

With that, he drew me in again and kissed me. This kiss was different from the last kisses. As though drinking thirstily from a glass of cool water, his full lips took me in and what felt like an undulation of tongue and lips began, our mouths encircling and riding against each other, our breaths the only break in a delicious sensation that seemed to go on and on, and yet, wasn't quite enough. We wanted more, both of us.

Our bodies grew hot against each other. As we pulled

closer, our remaining clothes became nuisances in the way. We wanted to feel and taste and to grind against firm bone and salty-tasting flesh.

"I'm afraid I can't be a gentleman anymore," Jeremy said, pulling back from me. He looked different now. His breathing had increased to the point where his chest was heaving in and out. His eyes had lost the soft, tender glow they'd had before, and now appeared more demanding and determined.

"You're so . . . big," I said, about the penis I felt growing larger against me.

"Ah, it's all smoke and mirrors," he whispered jokingly, and I laughed, so turned on that I was gasping, panting.

He pulled up my skirt so that it was up above my waist, panties exposed. After unzipping his cords, he took both his hands and placed them in a firm grip on either side of my waist. I felt small in his grasp as he gently lifted me onto his hardness, filling me with instant satisfaction.

"Why don't you play me a little," I heard him whisper.

I could not control the sounds that followed. As I pumped my body against his, eager for us to find our ecstasy together beneath the Prague moon, I let out cry after cry of pleasure and began to moan as though I myself were an instrument he was playing, finding its own song.

His shadowed face came closer. "Can we just . . . slow down?" he asked in a whisper. He then pulled far enough away to look at me, his brown eyes squinting, as though he wanted to tell me something.

He moved in and out between my legs, slowly pacing himself, now growing even harder and making me wait. When he moved this way, I could feel every part of his length and I could tell that he was gaining even better access to me. And then he suddenly stopped.

"Why won't you look at me, Danielle?"

"I am," I said, making sure that I was really looking at him now. Perhaps I'd glanced away, but only for a second. What did it matter?

He blinked at me, eyes becoming more intense. His irises were nearly black. I couldn't tell what he was thinking. It wasn't like Natasha's stares, which were simply a way of getting my full attention. This was different. It was as though with each passing moment our eyes were locked, Jeremy was peeling off my layers. The frightening thing was, the longer he stared, the less there seemed to be of me.

I felt trapped. I'd begun to feel empty and couldn't face the shame of looking into his eyes anymore. I turned my face away from him, and forced a deep breath.

"You found me out," I said. "I'm not like you." I closed my eyes. They had begun to tear up and I didn't want him to see. "Sorry," I whispered.

The moment now gone. I could feel his sex diminishing between my legs. But he didn't pull out just yet. Instead, he stroked my hair away from my eyes and tenderly kissed their lids.

"It's okay," he said. "I'll wait for you."

The following day, Jeremy and I were sitting on the patio of a local café, having lattes. A local cat was licking up the remains of a tub of yogurt beneath our table. She proudly began to pose for us, brushing her back against our legs. I brought out my camera, asking for her attention. She then looked away, preferring to function in her own space and time.

Just then Natasha walked past. As she looked at us, Jeremy—paying her no attention—gripped a large handful of my hair tightly and tilted my head back as far as it would go. "Does this feel good?" he asked.

I was now viewing Natasha upside down, as white sunlight hit my eyes, like a flashlight in a tunnel. I remembered her—the other night when she had undressed on my bed, and what my feelings for her had been.

"Yeah," I whispered to Jeremy. "It hurts a little, but in a good way." Natasha looked right through me and continued on, as though she did not recognize me. I wanted to call after her, to see where she was going, to remind her that I was still waiting for her, but something in me froze. I sat up and ran my hands over my face, rubbing my eyes, tired from last night.

"People are a lot like cats," I said to Jeremy, "eager to expose themselves as long as it's not required. They like to be in control."

"Then why don't you break the mold? Stay with me for the year, let things unfold as they will."

"Oh, well, I . . ." I hesitated, a sudden sadness coming over me. I realized that what had happened with Jeremy might have been selfish on my part, merely a result of my eagerness to forget my other troubles. It seemed I'd used Jeremy in the same way Natasha had used me.

"Listen," he said, resting his hand on mine, perhaps sensing my apprehension, "you don't have to explain. It was just an idea."

He reached into his knapsack and pulled out a CD. There was a picture of him on the cover, sitting on train tracks, holding his sax. His expression was peaceful and content. I tucked the CD into my camera case and thanked him.

"My information is inside. You can always reach me through my E-mail. I think you'll like the CD. I wrote all the songs."

"I know," I said.

We hugged and said good-bye, and he kissed me on both

cheeks as they do in Europe, then finally pressed his lips to mine. I thought about what he'd said to me the night before, words like *love* and *waiting*, and wondered if he felt embarrassed by that now, if he felt he'd said too much.

And then he whispered to me that I was "subterranean," a word I had never even heard before in the context of a person, and that I would later clarify with a dictionary as meaning one who develops underground, as opposed to living on the surface.

I couldn't tell if it would be good-bye for the day, or good-bye for the rest of my stay in Prague. Either way, it wasn't good-bye forever—that I knew for sure. I'd heard before that there were several words for good-bye in French, and just now I was glad neither of us spoke that language, glad we didn't have to discern what type of good-bye we were having.

Although Jeremy had played it very cool, he looked a little sad as he walked away, his head hanging lower than before. Wordlessly, he glanced back at me and purred like a cat— something that embarrassed me, although I liked his animal nature and that he could always be himself.

I almost regretted his leaving—or was it that I regretted having met him? I grieved not just for the loss, but also for the gain—the weight of knowing him, which I would now have to carry alone.

What he'd said about passion was true. It could wake the neighbors.

I restricted my photography to women and their bodies: there would be no more landscape. I had a responsibility to my truest passion now and I needed to focus.

I met women at the bus station, at cafés, in the halls of Charles University, at the newsstand. I was no longer afraid to initiate conversation with women, as I had been before. I was looking them in the eyes now and to my surprise, they were much more sympathetic. They smiled and greeted me. I smiled back and asked if they would be interested in modeling. Most women were flattered and said yes.

We would usually go to their place, so they felt more comfortable. I offered to pay the models thirty American dollars for the hour, as well as send them prints of the film. I demanded one thing of the models: that they did not pose. To help avoid this happening, I requested that they feel free to speak to me while I shot.

If they were quiet and stiff, or found difficulty in relaxing, I asked them about their fantasies. To my surprise they confessed—not just with words, but also with their bodies.

Their arms stretched open and they revealed their hearts. Breast shapes marked youth, strength, and experience. I found certainty in the sharp angles, and inspiration in the curves.

Legs uncrossed to unmask their sex: I saw inside of them. Vaginas appeared like open wounds—pink and bloodless. Incarnadine labias and clitorises, as expressive as a woman's lips—extroverted or concealed.

The bodies, all of them, fascinated me. With my viewfinder, I'd slowly climb their torsos until I reached their eyes—the echoes of the mind's desires, even those of my own mind.

My camera was becoming my mirror, and I was no longer afraid to look.

I hadn't forgotten about Jeremy, the comfort I had felt in his presence. But comfort seemed like betrayal to me now, in the midst of all this chance. I was still restless and felt myself at the precipice of understanding myself, knowing what to do with all the new feelings that swarmed inside of me like bees—a colony of desire searching for a hive.

My camera was many parts of me now—my eyes, my sex, and even my spine as it gave me purpose and strength. I began to purchase more magazines, fashion as well as erotic. I studied centerfold spreads, loaded film, and arranged the settings almost unconsciously, with an ease I never had before. My focus held me upright and I drew closer to my subjects. I saw deep inside of them. I saw that I wasn't alone.

I had a session at the apartment of a woman named Eva and shot her spread out on her mattress in a pair of lavender lace panties, making her thin body appear more voluptuous than it was.

"I need some sex," Eva hollered in English. Many locals could speak English quite well, but Eva wasn't as good with the accent as most other Czechs were.

Her platinum hair was an extreme contrast to her skin, as her cheeks blushed a burnt rose hue from the stuffiness of her upstairs flat—a tiny room that had only one small window.

"That shouldn't be hard to find," I answered, not knowing what other information to offer to appease her longing. She was beautiful, after all.

"You know," she said. "I take medication for my sex drive. For a while it was uncanny. I was after women." She let out a silly barreled laugh, covering her mouth.

I took a picture of her like this.

"Do you think you might just prefer women?" I asked.

"You mean am I ho-mo-sec-shew-all?" she asked crudely, breaking the word into syllables. "No, I'm sick! I want to fuck anything that moves. Not kidding. Even old man from church," she said, running out of air as though exhilarated. "I finally admitted to my mother and she took me to doctor. He put me on medication. Without it, I am nympho. I avoid alcohol or drugs because it cancel my medication."

After the shoot, she handed me a flyer from a place called Club Cibulka—some sort of trance music party up on the mountain. "It's a type of rave, open to the public. A good place to go crazy when you need."

"*Turn your interior lights on,*" the caption read.

"I go crazy many times there," Eva said. "Best place in Prague."

It took me two and a half hours to find it—first traveling by streetcar. Obnoxious teens dangled along the handrails of the trolley, shrieking back and forth to each other in a primitive way, jiggling the rails with all their strength, until the entire cart shook—some contest to see who could make the most waves. They made me think of gorillas at the zoo, and when they finally arrived at their stop, I half expected them to exit on all fours.

When I arrived at my stop, I began the rest of the journey by foot, walking alone in the near dark and asking locals for directions whenever I came across anyone (everyone seemed to know where Cibulka was). The roads to Cibulka were mysterious, paved in brick, and at other times, just laid in dirt, sometimes emerging to a frightening end with a broken staircase or fallen bridge. The edges of these roads were sometimes wide enough for a car, and then at other times, so narrow as to suit only someone traversing on foot. And then a car would pass me after I'd walked through one of these long stretches and climbed a staircase! Many things unanswered.

A pitch-black dirt road eventually led to a barn. *Club Cibulka*, a sign read. It was risky to have gone there, alone at night. But for the obsessed, passion trumps risk every time.

Once I'd finally arrived, it was easy to spot her.

Natasha was standing in the center of the barn beneath a swirl of traffic lights and disco balls, smiling as she spun. Her eyes were closed, her body reacting to the most dreadful music I had ever heard—if one could call it music. I could hear spoken word samples of children learning to count, in Czech, dubbed over fast techno drum beats and strange organ chords that sounded like something played at a vampire's ball.

Natasha was the only person dancing.

Had this been the place where she'd been spending all her evenings?

There was a line of people drinking, waiting to draw a drink from a phalanx of kegs. They seemed to be more intent on drinking than anything else, and no one seemed to be paying any attention to Natasha. Perhaps this was how she preferred to be—lonely, but not alone.

She hadn't spotted me yet. I was standing off to one side, and her eyes were still closed.

I closed my eyes, too, but only to compose a fantasy of slinking up behind her and pressing my body against the back of hers, wrapping my arms around her waist and kissing the back of her neck. I imagined burying my head in her hair, smelling her sweet fragrance. She wouldn't even have to look back to know it was me. She would turn, eyes still closed, and embrace me, our lips finding each other's. As the colored lights alternated and the music bled from one song to the next, our kiss would linger on, my mouth tingling against hers, my head dizzy with hope. Her kiss would say everything I wanted to know: how she felt about me, about herself, and about us.

But fantasy always collides with reality. When I finally opened my eyes, all I could see was an empty dance floor. Natasha was gone.

I was beginning to wonder if she had ever really been there.

Chapter 9

Night Gallery

For our poetry final, each of us was required to bring a bottle of wine to the old Jewish graveyard and read our poetry aloud. We met at midnight. Headstones dated back to 1307. Brick-paved paths were overgrown with grass that spread into the dark cracks. It was a tiny graveyard, crowded with over twelve thousand graves.

Natasha wore her Delilah blue shirt and a garland in her hair. She appeared more energetic than I had seen her in weeks. She flashed an occasional glance my way as we wandered through the paths, following Friedlander. She was still the one living in the shrine of my heart. I knew I could not succeed in dismantling this shrine until I had, at least, left Europe.

Friedlander spoke of poetry as severed images, wrested from their lived chaos, and of the idea of economy and how it plays a role in poetry. "Artists have a limited space to work with: a line. This line, this measured agenda, creates the alchemy of desire."

Wending through the shadowy yard, Friedlander lectured with a profound tone, melodious and nearly a stage whisper, as he explained about the death all artists must face with their thoughts and passions. "Words change in meaning once put to paper. The sacrifice they suffer forever alters their chemistry and sound. It is nearly impossible to capture the truth of anything. That is the great goal of every artist, but also the great mystery, and we must all learn to embrace and accept it, or we'll drive ourselves mad," he said.

The idea fascinated us. I was especially intrigued in view of how all art seemed to parallel in theory, whether it be poetry, photography, or the art of simply living. The transformation I'd undergone these past weeks had allowed me to let the subjects I photographed finally penetrate my lens. My photography was reborn, wildly alive—a form I was learning to welcome.

After, Friedlander led us on his tour of the yard, pointing out with a flashlight all the famous men who were buried there—Moses Beck and Rabbi Lowe—and that because the Jews had been given such limited space to bury their dead, many bodies had been buried on top of each other, causing lopsided tombstones that formed unruly, yet poetic-looking groups. Haunted by the images, I took several pictures using my flash.

After a period of silence, we all gathered beneath a section of large oaks, wide trunks that we could lean against. We uncorked our bottles of wine and began to read.

Mee Jun had written a melancholy poem about her daughter, and how she missed her daughter's odor. "Odor," Mee Jun said, looking up from her sheet of paper and around at the dark faces in the group. "Is this the word you use?"

For Valerie's final, she read a poem about bringing plastic flowers for the dead. About a long African millipede, black with a red head and black legs. Concentration camp images.

She wrote of how society seemed to take away our chances for happiness—and although she was speaking of the Jews, I felt she was speaking directly to me as she read.

Thus far during the term, I hadn't read anything aloud, and had slid by on the contingency that I would make up for it at the final. Friedlander had permitted this, "not because you are a beginning poet, but because we all have our own working style." I hoped I wouldn't have to read tonight as well.

Natasha offered to read next. She stood up and walked over to a headstone, laying an offering of flowers at its base before she began. She pulled out a thick yellow pad and began to read. Her poems were bountiful—she'd been working.

One was about John Lennon. "A god chasing its tail," she'd said, twisting the images in our minds. Another poem recounted images from the Louvre. "Did Vermeer's domesticated women dream of Turkish baths or sylphic evenings beneath a moon?"

She had digested much more than she had let on during our travels, proving that she required less time than I did to gather information and be moved and affected by it. She was the true poet of the group, and it was obvious that she had the most talent. She had, as Friedlander had allowed, her "own working style."

She never mentioned the *Mona Lisa*.

I nervously read a poem by May Sarton, feeling a bit ridiculous to have ever thought I could have somehow had something to offer a class of poets. I could only hope that they would be as open as I had learned to be, in seeing that the expression of art, so long as it was made, was interchangeable, and need not only be expressed through a restricted form. With this in mind, I then shared some photographs, using Friedlander's flashlight. I spread the matte papers across the grass, illuminating them one by one with the light, making a mock slide show. I'd decided to share a couple of the very graphic ones. Valerie raised her brows at the shots of women.

"Now we know why they call it the Velvet City," Valerie said, and everyone followed her comment with a laugh, including myself. Everyone except for Natasha.

"It's objectification," Natasha said.

The group went quiet. I somewhat expected this reaction, especially from Natasha, but now that it was here I had no way of protecting myself, other then letting my art speak for itself.

"When it comes to art, what isn't objectification?" I said, glancing over at Mee Jun, who held her hands clasped together. "It's like what Friedlander was saying about economy and passion—seeing things for the parts, rather than the whole—and why I think photography and poetry are so similar."

"Those shots are nothing like poetry," Natasha said, kicking up a little dust with her sandal and glaring at me now. She seemed disgusted with me.

"Good," Friedlander said, softening the blow a little. "Good. I was hoping for more conflict out of this group, actually. Really. Rejection is a good sign for the artist. It means you did something original. Bravo!"

The class applauded for me and I, awkwardly, accepted it with a nod. I didn't know what else to do or say, and as long as Natasha was upset, I could feel no real pride.

"It's pornography!" Natasha said, continuing.

"Hold it now," Friedlander said. "Let's not go there, dear poet. Our ability to speak freely has come too far to descend back into harangues about censorship."

Friedlander was not satisfied, however, with the amount of participation from me. He wanted more.

"Now, what about the poetry, Danielle?" he asked.

"I could read something else by . . ." I fumbled through my leather tote for something else I could read.

"Original *words*," he said. "Since that's what this course was about. I expect it from everyone. Even you."

I had nothing. I leaned down and gathered up the pictures that were spread across the grass, my camera lightly pressing against my chest as I moved. "I haven't written anything," I admitted.

"I don't believe that. You must have thought of something while you were here and written it down. I don't care if you have to read the back of a postcard you wrote to your mother or make something up on the spot. No one passes without reading original work."

There were some notes. I had written something down a few weeks back. It had been about a dream. But it was all I had. I looked around, caught a glance of Natasha, looking at me. I saw a fearless woman standing before me, a woman strong in her convictions, even if they were different from mine. The most beautiful thing about Natasha, I realized, was that she had a faith, a stance, despite the fact that most of the class disagreed with her.

Her pride and unwillingness to compromise gave me the permission I needed to be myself.

My heart raced as I opened up my bag and brought out the piece of paper.

For the first time in my life, I knew whose call I was answering.

RESCUE ME
by Danielle Webber

The wind carries my pride away in pieces
Sandy fragments of the body, breast, and eye

Life abroad, disconnected to the torso
I must refrain from taking back
what is not mine.
Take pieces of me, then, collect them
What's gone is this way not forgotten,
I'll make photographs with what is left
Where not even darkness will escape.

Afterwards, feeling more exposed than I ever had, I threw my camera against the concrete, the loud crack reverberating like a breaking bone.

"That was the most idiotic post-punk thing I've ever seen," Natasha said. We were heading back towards our room. The final was over, as well as the term. Somewhere, within the depths of the night, Natasha had decided to talk to me again. I didn't know why, so I just let it happen and agreed to walk back to the room with her.

"Things like that don't mean much when you have money," she said, trying to pick a fight. "You'll just go buy another camera."

I ignored the comment.

We walked along the river and across the Charles Bridge toward the castle. There was a drunken couple standing near the bridge, embraced in a kiss. I thought this spectacle would disgust Natasha, so I quickly looked away, toward the ground. But she surprised me by grabbing my hand.

Although it was now cold outside, her hand was amazingly warm. Touching her again felt surreal, a moment I'd anticipated for so long that the reality of it almost numbed me, and I could barely feel her skin against mine, save for its heat.

By now, it was early morning, not yet light. The shimmering river reflected the street lamps, making the refracted lights appear alive and buzzing like insects. Impressions like this seemed to happen when I was tired or drunk, and this morning I was some of both.

"This view is so Kafka-esque," Natasha said. "Beautiful, but in a strange way. I can't escape it."

Natasha unclasped her hand from mine and offered me a cigarette, mimicking the accents of the French women at the Moulin Rouge. "Cigar, cigarette," she said.

I grinned and took one. It took me a moment to get the lighter to work, chuckling a little at the instant thought of Grant seeing me smoke—a disgusting act of self-sabotage, no doubt, in his mind. I lit the cigarette and took a fast drag, coughing a little.

"But you know what?" Natasha began, blowing out a gust of creamy smoke. "You've inspired me to let go of the things that weigh me down. I might not write anymore after this trip. Not much more, anyway."

"That doesn't sound like inspiration," I said. "You must be joking."

She made no comment.

"Decisions like this don't mean much when you're a dramatist," I joked, mocking her previous comment. "You'll change your mind tomorrow. You have too much talent not to."

"But I don't want to be talented," she said, pausing to take another long drag. "I don't want to be an artist, you see. I just want to be normal and happy. I'm sick of trying to 'carry the weight of the world on my shoulders', as Friedlander says. My own life should matter more—it's heavy enough to carry."

She gestured out towards the river and the lights. "Look at all this stuff. I'll never even see it again. And it's so much more important than poetry."

She stopped in the street and looked at me, really looked at me. Now that we were no longer moving, I felt naked again, as I had with her in the beginning, and then again on the train after Paris, only this time this feeling of transparence gave me a rush of exhilaration rather than fear. I could smell the sandalwood again. The witchy fragrance of her skin had grown into a familiar, if not essential, stimulant to me.

"How can you give up your dream so easily?" I asked.

She smiled and I noticed the tiny lines around her eyes already beginning to form. Nineteen years and she was old. She was the kind of woman who would show her age early, but for some reason I found this to be another of her charms.

"Who says it was ever my dream?" she said, bringing a hand up through her hair. "I refuse to be a parody of a poet, or to live a so-called poetic life for the sake of mimicry. If my life happens to fall into the lines of artistry, let it only be for reasons that come as naturally as the way I run my fingers through my hair, hoping no one is watching."

"That's beautiful."

"I've put so many years into my hair that I'll never have the guts to cut it," she said. "I feel handicapped by it. Sometimes I've wished that I was one of those people whose hair just stops growing at a certain point. In fact, sometimes I wish *everything* would stop changing and I could just relax and live. I don't want to worry anymore. Worrying isn't living." She took my hands, both of them, and ran them up through the sides of her hair, close to her scalp. "Feel all this?" she said. "It's not really red. I've been dying my hair so long that I can't even remember my natural color. Sometimes I have nightmares that I forgot to color it and I wake up to a full head of gray hair."

A small wind picked up and we began to walk again, silently for a while. I thought about her with gray hair and how different it would make her, both inside and out. It might help her understand herself, and enable her more exoticism.

"I'd like to love you." I was surprised I said this.

She glanced at me and raised a sultry brow, throwing the smoldering butt of her cigarette down. "You say that as though you've never done it."

"I mean *love*. You know, the gushy tied-down kind that people break each other's hearts over." I brought my cigarette to my lips and took a last drag. "I want that. But only if it comes as naturally as the way I run my fingers through my hair, hoping no one is . . ."

She stopped me and pulled me close and kissed me, her lips firm. It felt important, like a first kiss—or perhaps a last. When we pulled apart, she smiled and began to walk again.

"You like my words, don't you?"

"You're a fantastic poet," I said. "A great visionary."

"You're wrong. My mom's the visionary," she said. "Straight out of *The Hobbit*. She can visualize anything. It's me who can't. I'm a romantic. I see things one way. I want the dream. The whole white wedding, house with a picket fence and two children . . . I don't know if it will work, though. There's a part of me that feels I'll end up divorced some day, maybe even twice." She laughed and sighed. "That would devastate me."

"If you know so much, why go there?" I asked, somewhat afraid of the effects my question might have upon her. She answered with ease, as though she'd already rehearsed her answer long before I had ever asked the question:

"Because, I'm a slave to society," she said rather comically, tilting her head to one side. "I admit it. I want to fit in with everyone else. Poetry is my great escape, which is why I need to keep it like that. I shouldn't have to work at being a poet. That destroys its beauty."

"What about your knight in shining armor?" I asked. "You didn't meet him this summer, like your psychic predicted. Does that devastate you?"

"No," she said casually. "I'll just find another psychic."

A group of young girls passed us, all beautiful and brown-skinned with long shiny black hair and almond eyes.

"Hello," they greeted us, eager to use their English.

"Hi." We smiled back.

The group was from somewhere far away, Middle Eastern, perhaps. Maybe Muslim, since there were two older women following them, both wearing burkahs. It was odd how being away from home for just eight weeks could make me feel so comfortable around strangers.

"I'm craving an ice cream sandwich. Where could I find one at this time?" Natasha asked.

"That store might be open," I said, pointing up ahead to a little market that was sometimes open late at night.

The corner store was open and we got the ice cream and took it over to a bench. We still had a long walk back to the room, and the ice cream was a great excuse to rest.

"Uh! I could never be a lesbian," Natasha said, taking a big mushy bite and swallowing. "Women are too complacent. I'd get fucking fat."

"I adore your decadence. I don't prefer thin," I said.

"But *you're* thin!" she screamed.

"I know," I said. "But I eat."

"Only around others," she said, licking her lips. "That's what skinny people do. Go to greasy spoons and order the most disgusting items on the menu—chicken-fried steak, mashed potatoes and gravy, buttermilk biscuits and gravy—and down it all in front of us as if it were part of your regular routine so we think your beauty comes naturally."

"You are too much."

"Sometimes—even to myself," she agreed.

"You look really adorable with the smudge of ice cream on your chin," I said. "My mother would die if she knew I became a lesbian on her money."

The sun began to rise bright and pink. We wanted to get back to our room quickly, so we hailed a taxi. Outside, along the passing apartments, people had strung up little stained towels of orange and mint green and yellow. The city was silent, and Natasha began to whisper the words to her song. *The air seemed to me light . . . With colors of an infinite softness . . .*

Why seek perfection when there was so much to be found in the imperfections? The chance that this moment would never come again made every part of it the more sacred. Expectations set aside, we severed ourselves from the world and embraced what was left between us. If I couldn't be myself, who would be me? Being myself had become a crucial responsibility I could no longer ignore. It was this powerful realization that opened me inside, fully, with a type of surrender I had never experienced. Denying Natasha would not have been possible.

Back inside our room, I lay next to her, both of us naked except for our panties. I stroked the beauty mark on her back—a back that once scorned me, turned from me in denial. Now, rolling on top of my body, she accepted me.

My lips encircled only her softest areas: behind her ears, the palms of her hands, and along her thighs. The recording in my head came back again, my voice reminding me to take my time, because there is only this one moment and no guarantees for tomorrow. All I could do was give all of myself, and leave no place undiscovered.

Being in Natasha's arms, nestled in her beauty, I became freer, more beautiful, not unlike her in some ways.

I played with her nipples until they stood up hard and erect. My fingers ran down along the outside of her pink lace panties. I could feel her hair through the lace and the coarseness made me weak with desire, desperate to get closer. I kissed along the sides of the panties and around the edges where the panties bordered. I took her by her waist and slid her underwear down her body—slow enough to feel the slight growth of hair now on her legs, which gave a pleasurable friction to the touch.

There is no room for self-consciousness when making love to a woman. No pretensions that work. Positions and poses that previously had turned men on and brought them into climax had done nothing for me. Now, with a woman, there was a shared ecstasy, the moment more than just an erotic accident. Pleasing Natasha was a pleasure for me, too, and made everything seem new. I relaxed into her body; our breathing found a synchronicity, our bodies drawing closer. We gladly gave and received, managing both pleasures at once. It all happened effortlessly.

I wasn't afraid this time to lunge my tongue straight into her. Once inside, I realized that I had never truly made love to a woman until that instant. Inside I found a woman entirely exposed and responsive to my every move. *I had all of her . . .*

Her taste immediately drew me back to the last time we had been together, a reminder that this was merely a continuance of that moment and that no separation or break had ever occurred. How familiar her body was to me, that deep sandalwood intoxication, mixed with her feminine musk. *I had never forgotten . . .*

Natasha brushed my hair back with her hand and I could feel her eyes looking down, watching me. I closed my eyes tighter and gripped both her thighs, spreading them wider so that no part of her body would go unnoticed or untouched. There would be no second thoughts this time—no regrets or moments I wished I would have back. There she was, spread out before me like an open sky, arching her back high, and I wasn't afraid to look.

I pulled her into me and began to make love to her with my tongue. I watched her swell wide and pink as I moved.

"Oh, God!" she whispered.

Her perfume was sweet and fertile, and I cupped my mouth over her, and sucked as though she had a small penis. This sent Natasha into a delirium of moaning as she buried her hands into my hair.

"Don't stop. Don't stop!" she commanded.

I continued back and forth between her well of wetness and her little crest of skin until all became silent and I found myself wedged between the grasp of her thighs, unable to move.

She rocked in firm contractions that became harder each time, her strength and power building. It was like being seduced by a snake. She started slow, and within seconds I was locked so tightly inside the hold of her body that I realized it was impossible for me to break free. Her thighs squeezed. My mouth still open wide, I could barely find air, and I shifted myself enough as a way to try to catch my breath, but it wasn't soon enough. The rocking had increased, my wet cheek against her pubic hair as she bucked into a fitful ride of ecstasy that whirled me to a place where words had no meaning, and her cries of pleasure were the only sounds I wanted to hear.

Afterwards, I slid up next to Natasha, onto the pillows, and she held me in her arms. We both took in lungsful of air, our bodies shining with perspiration. I leaned down into her neck and licked her tangy skin, then I pulled my underwear down and guided her fingers inside of me.

All the nerves in my body felt exposed, electric to her touch. No one had ever felt so good.

I opened my knees. "Yes," I whispered, as she pressed her finger way up inside of me.

Her touch was different than I'd remembered. More aggressive. Quickly she replaced her fingers with her mouth and caressed me with her tongue—agreeing, disagreeing, loyal to my tides of movement. I opened farther, convulsing as her tongue took flight. Then she crawled on top of me, our bodies mashing together once again. She set her lips on mine and our tongues twisted together, our sweet scents mixing. The tickling, energetic sensation started inside me as we moved, the wetness between our bodies thick. My body writhed upwards with each press against me, causing me to shudder.

She continued to wrap herself around me, the weight of her body against mine, light and soft, yet full of curves and landscape. The mass of her clitoris was just enough to send me gasping.

"I'm a man, aren't I?" she asked, mouth buried in my neck.

"Hell, no," I said. "You're a goddess."

After, we lay still, and for such a long time, unable to get up and dress or even to talk. We didn't fall asleep right away, but lay there, embracing one another, stroking each other's hair.

Although the word "love" had never meant much to me, it had come to mean something with Natasha. It stood as a whole feeling, not abridged and economical, like a photo of a house or a building, but something wide and internal, something I didn't have to express with words or a photo, just acknowledge. And seeing Natasha's face just then, soft and tired from our lovemaking, seemed an endless indulgence.

I took off my bracelet, the silver one I'd purchased at the Louvre, and clasped it around her wrist, hoping it might somehow lock what was between us.

Chapter 10

Radical Miles

I returned to my old life the same way I had left it: photography felt lifeless again. I'd lost my inspiration. My artistic freedom abroad had only been a substitute for something else, camouflaging the memory of something dormant. Now I knew I was alone.

I'd passed the summer class, despite my having written only one poem. Friedlander must have also made exceptions for wounded hearts, I think.

My mother's home was no longer familiar to me. I removed the postcards from my bedroom mirror, the black and white images I'd collected for years of women in Paris with bobbed hair and cloche hats, pearls dangling between petite breasts and ladies salsa-dancing together amidst a ballroom of men. I was now aware of the pedestrian nature of such things, of the futility of trying to appreciate these images before ever experiencing them—of loving a woman. Now these images meant something to me, these stark vintage photographs of women in shadowy light. I refused to confine their legacy to gimmicky nostalgia, no matter how much I loved looking at them. The only mementos from my travels I would keep would be the Moulin Rouge cassette from Natasha and the small Eiffel Tower model I had purchased at the souvenir shop. My reasons for choosing this particular bauble extended beyond my stay in Paris—the memento was an amulet that repelled fear and a magnet that drew me closer to liberty.

I felt like a stranger in Los Angeles, so I began to photograph my surroundings as though they were new to me. And then, slowly, after a few weeks had passed, I began to accept them again as my own. What little mystery had acquired in my absence soon faded back to normalcy. It seemed my best work would come from when I was separated from routine, from the place I came from.

From time to time, I would open a European cuisine cookbook and prepare full meals for Mother and myself, trying to repeat some of the rich dishes I'd eaten in Europe. Mushroom soufflé with brandy sauce, summer squash sautéed with herbs, pear salad, and tarte au chocolate. I wanted to share this pleasure. Cooking seemed to help my mood a little, but Mother was as resistant to my efforts as ever, her motivations still governed by necessity rather than pleasure. "Why bother," she would say, entering the now sweet-smelling kitchen, her hands on her hips, "when it's only you and me?"

Up in my bedroom I'd play the Moulin Rouge cassette, each song now nostalgic to me, despite my previous indifference to the music. Some nights I would recall early fantasies I'd had of touching Natasha, her breasts, how her clothes could not hide the weight of her curves. With my eyes closed, I evoked the slight detailed marks left on them as a result of her body growing too quickly in her youth, so quickly that her skin could not stretch fast enough.

On campus I would see her, standing in the latticework of light, chatting with other students, her face seemingly always to the sun. I wished I could get closer, if only to take in her

fragrance and smell the familiar oil she wore on her skin—
that woody smell that had instantly transported me to pleasure.

But something had changed. I could tell that she had
moved, that she had changed her direction. Her clothes were
not as bright. The women in the circle around her seemed more
conservative—popular girls and sorority types who shaved their
legs every morning and called each other before class to ask
what the others were wearing.

Natasha seemed washed, her past forgotten, her legs
smoothly shaved again. Detachment was essential to her style
of living, a life empty of self-reflection. I persuaded myself
that despite this cool veneer, the deepest part of her would always be there—the rich, murky part boiling under the surface, occasionally revealed through poetry, lovemaking, or the
songs she chose to sing at the top of faraway bridges.

When I rubbed my wrist, I noticed the empty spot where
the silver bracelet used to be. We'd known each other in some
way that was now closed. She was now who she had always
been—everything that was different from me, someone who
I would never know.

I had fallen in love with her shadow.

"Rescue yourself," I wanted to whisper in Natasha's ear.

My eyes turned again to what lay before me and I continued on my way.

Several months went by. And then one afternoon in mid-
fall, I received a letter:

Danielle,
Finally I am in a place to write you. After I returned from
Prague, I had a crash and almost took my own life. Then I

got some help and learned that I could no longer live as I was, and that if I wanted to be a mother to my daughter, and to be happy, I would have to change.

Since this time, I have many things to be happy about. I have fallen in love. With Tokyo! I moved here with my daughter and I am supporting us on my own for the first time. I am working in a gentlemen's club during the day, called Tantric, which pays well, and at night I am with my daughter and an English tutor comes and teaches us lessons. I think my English is improving! I began as a hostess at Tantric, and then became a dancer. Can you believe, at my age? My life is not yet respectable in the eyes of my family, but my daughter is happy and that is more important. For me, I am having a life I never believed I could have. I thought it was too late for what I now have. Changing countries is a large step, but being true to myself is even greater.

At Tantric, I take off my clothes when I dance, and men see me as I am. They like me. They like my age and that I am a mother. Some customers come in just to see me. And some customers are very nice and sweet. I could kiss them but I don't! They have a lot of security at Tantric. One of the bouncers is named Abe and he wants to marry me. He is a clown and everyone loves him. On his breaks, he comes inside to watch me dance and I give him a special show. He asks why I don't have a husband and I say, why do I need one? I am still waiting for an answer.

This club has no mirrors. The owner says the customers are mirrors and I have learned to like it because I can forget my age. Most girls who work at Tantric are young and look like models but my knowledge of Chinese makes me popular with customers and also, they say, my smile.

I want you to know that you have been my inspiration. I saw you grow over the summer like a flower.

I think you are a great artist and a beautiful woman.
I wish you love.

Mee Jun

Included with the letter was a photo of Mee Jun, standing in front of a staircase, harlequin wallpaper behind her and a crystal chandelier above. She was smiling flirtatiously with her arm around a bouncer, who I assumed was Abe, and looking great in a low-cut cocktail dress and heels. Her hair was in a ponytail and, strangely, she appeared years younger. She could pass for being in her twenties now.

It was amazing what happiness could do for a person.

After reading the letter, I locked my bedroom floor, buried my face into my pillows, and cried harder than I had in years—coughing and gasping for breath. The last time I had cried this way was when I was a girl and my mother, unbeknownst to me, had taken my cat of nine years to the pound while I was at school. My father had just left her and she had decided my cat was just one too many responsibilities for her at that time. I'd come home from school to find Mittens gone forever. I hadn't even gotten to say good-bye to her.

What was the parallel? Why did I feel so taken from again? The letter from Mee Jun left me feeling so empty. Mee Jun was truly living now, no longer allowing others to control whom she loved or whom she gave her time to. Hadn't I learned this last summer, or was the lesson unfinished? And Mee Jun had wished me love. Had I not found it over the summer, or had I let it be taken from me?

A person can only do so much to get what they want. After all, love is a consensual act, not a game of solitaire. Jeremy was, no doubt, smart enough to know this.

But was I?

Mother had gone to work and I had the house to myself. I grabbed my camera, a notebook, and a Coke, and made my way to the pool where I would spend the afternoon in the sunlight, before Mother's return. I wondered, walking onto the back patio, my bare feet against the dry pavement, what had happened to Mittens, if she had made it to another home or not. I closed my eyes for a moment and hoped that she did. It was all I could do for either of us.

Stretching out across the rattan recliner, the L.A. October sky a perfect hyacinth blue, I thought about Jeremy again. I opened my Coke and took deep sips of the cold bubbly liquid, remembering the kisses Jeremy gave me underneath the moon on that starry night in Prague, and the way he'd looked at me, differently from the way anyone ever had. I thought of him as he must be now: playing in some bluesy bar, shocking people with his lack of convention and his personal authority. Was he happy now? Did he meet others, like me, with whom he could smile and share his innermost thoughts? What were his days like?

I listened to the water lap against the edges of the pool, reminding me of the lagoons of Venice. Gazing at my empty bottle of Coke, I thought about the propositions given me over the summer. The good advice—and the not so good. And the moments that stayed with me most. I felt a pang of guilt and, on a whim, I made an oath: I would begin to recognize devotion. And never again would I let an infatuation stand in the way of something deeper.

I picked up my camera, removing the lens cap, and looked through the viewfinder at my feet. I let the camera travel up my leg and decided to remove my clothes. Setting the camera down, I began to undress, tossing my clothes in the pool. I decided to photograph them—deflating garments floating

atop the chlorine green, uninhibited by a body. Their lifeless-
ness both depressed and intrigued me.

Minutes later, I set my camera down on the tile near the
edge of the pool and dove in naked, immersed in the sensation of cool water rushing over my skin. Being underwater
was possibly the best feeling in the world to me: wet, everywhere, body fully extended, stretching to the earth's ends.

Pushing off the edge of the pool, I propelled myself through
the water, straight across the pool. I coasted as far as I could at
first, my hands above my head, body in a straight line. Then,
reveling in my own control, I placed my face in the water as I
began kicking, lifting it out only when I needed to breathe.
With my body relaxed, I fell into a natural, comfortable rhythm
as I swam, sliding my palms smoothly into the water, knowing that each stroke was contributing to the whole, and that I
had no reason to hurry.

After returning to the photography department, I received some acclaim for my summer's work. Although most
in the department preferred the more outrageous nude shots
of strangers I'd taken while in Prague, it was the quiet, sensitive shots of Natasha that I prized most.

For me, these shots lived and breathed, staring back at me,
beckoning my dormant self to step forward and admit that it
was now alive—admit it to the world.

Perhaps too eager to show my portfolio, I made my way
down to a prestigious Beverly Hills art gallery which had photography shows I have always admired. I brought a collection of
photos, mostly pictures of Natasha, and then a few landscape
shots from the cemeteries in Prague. The owner complimented
my "eye," but encouraged me to check back when my work
had matured.

"Show me more of Prague," I was advised. "I think you were on to something there."

Ironically, rather than showing her the outcome of my summer's awakening, I had shown her its catalyst.

I pulled out the CD and opened its case. Pushed "play" on my walkman. Sultry jazz began with a winding horn that sounded unlike any other horn in the world and made me smile. I was on a plane, returning to the Velvet City, and I wasn't even sure exactly why. But I trusted it. I trusted the art gallery's owner's few words. And I trusted the stirring inside of me which came as soon as I thought of returning.

Jeremy, with rosy cheeks and pale gray eyes, took me in his arms and drew me as close as he could. He smelled of brisk starry nights and moons, smoky bars, and pomade. He smelled like the other side of the world. And then he thanked me.

"Thank you. But for what?" I asked

"For defying your conventions," he said, pressing his lips to mine.

"How have I done that?" I asked, pulling back.

He gave me a sardonic look. "By writing to me." There was a pause. "I know I'm not your type."

His tongue entered my mouth with his next kiss. I began to feel warm and wet inside.

"You're not my *mother's* type," I corrected, then kissed him back.

He took his time, kissing me in all my treasured places, my neck, my chest, my belly, growing harder as he traveled my body.

"Mmm," I moaned, my hand caressing the outside of his pants, moving back and forth until his hard ridge stood at attention.

I leaned down and unzipped his fly, wanting to release him from his pants. He wasn't wearing any underwear. He pulled off his pants. I licked the base of him, and he shuddered.

Slowly, I began to caress his thighs with my mouth, gradually kissing up towards his hardness. I went back and forth, from one thigh to another, across his stomach, but careful not to lick his cock; this I skipped. Every time I passed over him he let out a gasp and a sigh, his rising excitement fueling me all the more. I kept up the teasing and he finally held my head in his palm, gripping either side of my head and trying to get me to take him into my mouth. But I wouldn't: I wanted this evening's fulfillment to come from inside of me, and for both of us at once.

My entire body seemed wet for his. Like a cat, I wanted to rub myself across his stomach, thighs, hands, and face. Our breathing increased. The landscape of his body had changed in the darkness. He'd become smoother, younger, more romantic. The sadness of his eyes had disappeared in the shadows. And I felt beautiful.

"Let's wake the neighbors," I said.

We didn't need to use our hands to guide ourselves. We were both so hungry, our bodies needing no coaxing. We craved each other and knew exactly what to do to satisfy the craving. Finally, he entered me and I gasped. It hurt perfectly.

"I'm not going to last very long," he whispered.

I thought, how wonderful to be given such tender damage by someone whom I adore, this intense coupling of love and pain.

As gentle as he tried to be, I screamed; then instantly, in

less than a second, there was no pain, and just as instantly, I wanted more of him. Within me, he searched for all places he could go deeper, all the places still untouched by his length. I rode him, screaming in his ear, until he let out a gasp and a whine, followed by such trembling silence that I thought he might be crying, his pelvis lifting high with each last thrust. And then, as though it had never happened, he was ready to go again.

The second catharsis came even more quickly than the first. We became curiously unsettled, smelling each other in a new way, making new sounds, and were soon carried by a riot of ecstasy such as I had never known.

It was mid-fall, but my summer had just begun.

I looked Jeremy in the eyes then, and saw there what I had so long feared to look at: my own reflection in the eyes of someone I truly respected.

Epilogue

He holds my jacket and purse, and I run into the fountain, allowing water to spray all over my dress, which sticks to my body as though I am wearing nothing. Despite my being in the center of a city park, I do not feel like hiding.

Water shoots up from the pipes and blasts against me. I am surrounded by wet strangers, mostly children, squealing and laughing, trying to cool themselves, or maybe just shake off the familiar.

Jeremy is holding my camera, film ready in a bag in case I am seized by inspiration. He watches me, grinning through his black sunglasses. Subterranean, he calls me.

The water surrounds me like rain. I like the feel of the cold drops against my forehead, face, arms, and hands. I tilt my head back, open my mouth, and let it fall onto my tongue. I wince a little, but welcome the rush because it is a beautiful day in Prague, and I have no idea what will happen next.

Many beliefs say that death is a mistake, a penalty for mankind, a price paid for our failures and weaknesses. People who hold these beliefs often whisper promises to the dying, just before the moment of separation comes, a last desperate hope to hang on.

The only way I can escape death, I believe, is to never live—to exist—without passion. I have died more than once, but I've learned to look forward to each rebirth. I see that a good life is made up of many deaths, and is about breaking promises and whispering no more.